WELCOME TO
BROOKVILLE

KELLY ENNIS

Printed in the United States of America
Print ISBN: 978-1-951490-78-2
eBook ISBN: 978-1-951490-79-9

Library of Congress Control Number: 2020923818

Published by DartFrog Plus,
the hybrid publishing imprint of DartFrog Books.

Publisher Information:
DartFrog Books
4697 Main Street
Manchester, VT 05255

www.DartFrogBooks.com

Join the discussion of this book on Bookclubz. Bookclubz is an online management tool for book clubs, available now for Android and iOS and via Bookclubz.com.

For my dog, Bella.

JANUARY 15-18

What sort of people would treat a human being like this? He had no idea. But then again, he wasn't a human being, was he? Not to them. To them, he was Patient J1518. If you were going to take someone off the street, deliberately blind him, dress him in old pajamas that someone had clearly worn before him, and keep him locked in a room where the only place to sleep was the floor, it was impossible to regard him as a human being. But a patient? Why not a prisoner? Because that was what he was. He couldn't go anywhere without their say-so, and his hands were handcuffed behind his back. Strange kind of patient if you ask him.

He had a backstory, of course. Anyone with a present has a past. In his case, it was thin and well on its way to disappearing. If he tried very hard, he could remember being in bed, a hospital bed, beside a woman he was pretty sure was his wife—but why they were together in a hospital was beyond him. He was wearing a mask, and he was fairly sure that his wife, if that was who she was, was wearing one, too. What came before that, how they got there, he couldn't remember.

He couldn't remember leaving the hospital, either, but he must have because the next thing he knew he was alone in a room—this room that was more prison cell than anything else.

Was that a memory? It seemed like a memory, but it could just as easily have been fiction created by a mind hungry for activity. And how long ago it took place, if a memory is what it was, God only knew. A year ago? A previous lifetime? How could you know how much time had passed when nothing happened and no one spoke and everything that made life real was absent?

But now it seemed that something was about to happen. He didn't know if he should be afraid, but what he did know was that action was better than neglect, words were better than silence, and if this was the end, then let it come.

When you have nothing, you have nothing to lose.

"Release." The voice was odd, distorted. Something you might hear at the other end of a train platform on a windy day. But he sensed that the door had slid open—sensed rather than heard because it was more like a shift in the silence than a sound. An inflow of air. He stood up cautiously, unaware of how long he had been sitting on the floor and uncertain how steady he was going to be on his feet. In any case, he couldn't see anything. He'd been able to see before he was brought here, but that was just one of the things that had been done to him. Though, it was possibly the worst so far.

He took careful, sliding steps, as if letting his foot fall from more than an inch above the floor would shatter his bones from toes to hip. He walked toward the place from which he could sense air flowing into the room, taking his time because he had no idea what he was walking toward. You'd have to be very trusting to move quickly in those conditions, and trust had seeped away in the uncounted hours waiting... And for what? He had no idea. Perhaps now he'd find out.

He couldn't see, nor could his hands take the place of the eyes they had stolen from him. But he could still hear, and at the moment he heard his own breath and the shuffle of his feet sliding forward. He could also feel, and apart from the tired PJs he wore, one of the things he felt was what held his mouth shut. It wasn't tape, but it was pressed tight against his face—not stuck to his skin, but held there by what felt like rubber bands. They tugged at the hair on the back and sides of his head, and when he flexed his jaw to try and dislodge the mask so he could speak, the rubber bands or straps or whatever they were pinched him. He'd stopped trying.

When they took away his eyes they didn't sew the eyelids shut, and he felt air moving in the sockets. It was as though the wind would whistle through his head and freeze his brain.

Whenever he wanted to say something, he foamed a little at the mouth, a thin trickle of drool seeping from beneath the mask and down his chin. He wanted to wipe his face, but couldn't.

The floor in the new room felt the same beneath his feet as it did in the old one, but he knew he had passed through a doorway. The shift in the air and the accompanying sounds had made that clear to him. Behind him, he heard the door close and felt the air shift again, puffing softly against his back. Someone was walking around him; was it the person who had shut the door? No—if he placed his trust in his ears (and he had nothing else to trust), he sensed someone behind him as someone else continued to circle him. There might have been others; there *were* others, or at least one more, because the two he had already sensed were breathing normally, but someone else had some kind of a cold and was sniffling nearby. Three, then.

Why did he think instinctively of them as men? Easy: he didn't want to think that women could behave this way. He probably needed to disabuse himself of that notion, though.

There was that feeling of being stared at. Was that something given to the blind in exchange for the loss of sight? Or was it imagined? The soft snickers he heard just then weren't in his head. He was being laughed at. And then something wet struck his cheek and he knew that he had been spat on. He stepped back, but bumped into whoever was behind him, who then pushed him forward with a scornful grunt. The force of it shoved a wheezing cough out of his lungs, and foam passed his lips, soaking into and around the mask over his mouth.

"Please," he said, but regretted it immediately when more foam came out. He spat with as much force as he could, terrified of choking, and then did so anyway. *Breathe through your nose if you want to go on living.* Although he wasn't sure he wished for that, he followed his own advice and took a deep breath. Smell—that turned out to be another sense that hadn't been taken from him, though what it was he smelled he could not have said.

At another push from behind, he fell against a cold tiled wall and yelped in pain as the impact drove his mask deeper into his face.

His shoulders were gripped and he was wrenched upright. There was a sharp pain in the palm of his left hand, as though he was being carved like a Thanksgiving turkey.

Once again he wondered what sort of people would treat a human being like this. Because that was a moan: a moan of pleasure. The doctor, if that was what he was, was taking pleasure in tearing apart someone else's flesh. The blind man didn't want to scream. That, surely, was what these people wanted. They cherished his suffering and he didn't want to give it to them. He tensed every muscle in his body to avoid the pain. The man thought he could take it, but deep inside he wanted to scream like someone in a horror movie.

And then the cutting stopped. His palm throbbed where it had been assaulted. "Hello, Simon," someone said.

Simon. That was his name; he remembered that. It had been so long since anyone called him by that name—or by any other for that matter—that he had almost forgotten it. Now it filled his mind. *Simon. Simon. My name is Simon.*

But when the voice said his name again, he realized something very strange. The voice he was hearing was his. He barely recognized it, but now it came rushing back to him. His name was Simon, and that was his voice, speaking inside his brain. It spoke calmly, with confidence. Simon tried to remember the last time he'd felt confident about anything. He couldn't. Had it ever happened?

"Wha?" Foam gathered around the edges of the mask again as he suffered another violent cough.

"Oh gosh, don't speak," his voice said. "That's a side effect of the drug those wonderful doctors gave you. Well, gave *us*." His voice paused, as if it wasn't sure what to say next. "I have to be honest; you don't look great."

The voice felt physically nearby, but also somehow buried deep inside his brain, as though a version of himself stood just behind him. He shivered a little, as one might when someone silently creeps up and grazes skin with a single fingertip.

"Listen to me, Simon." Did he have a choice? His head slumped, though he still stood with his back straight. He could feel his hand bleeding. "See, these doctors are not like other doctors. They stalked you, studied you, and looked after you for years on end. And they know." The voice paused for dramatic effect. "You're a sick man."

"I'm not!" Simon moaned the words into his mask, then hunched forward, coughing. "I'm not sick! I don't have anything!"

The silence that followed was pure and cold. It occurred to him that people with sight could not experience this kind of silence; their eyes always drew them to even the slightest sounds. Only in the dark did things become so very, very quiet.

"You've just been thinking about your past," said the voice. "Let's talk about your future. Or, your present. There are three mirrors right in front of you, Simon. We're going to make a choice together."

There was a pause, giving Simon a chance to wonder what kind of choices he could possible have in a place like this. Could he choose to leave and go home? Did he even remember where home was?

"It's the most important choice anyone could ever make," said the voice. "Isn't that exciting? What you're going to do—what we are going to do together—is decide how you're going to live. I'm not talking about in here, and we're not going to choose a house or an apartment for when you get out of this place. This is something much more fundamental. We're going to choose the lifetime you are going to live in. How many people do you suppose ever get to do that?"

What could this mean? Choosing a life to live?

Simon kept his mouth shut, but coughed again. The sharp bite of it made it feel like his chest was being sawed in half.

"I don't think we have ever met, me and you," the voice continued. "See, I am not you, but a part of you. I'm your sight. I have the power to see colors in your time."

Maybe he was sick after all. The sickness just wasn't physical. Here he was, imagining a part of himself—his eyesight, personified and talking to him. Its words seemed almost warm as they fluttered into his brain. Could the sight-voice hear what he was thinking? Or could he hide from it? It seemed unlikely.

"Let me take you somewhere, Simon. It's a very familiar place. You will not remember everything, but we'll see if you can recall any part of what happened that night. Now, walk into the mirror on the left."

How was a blind man supposed to know where the mirror on the left was? Except—obviously—that it was on the left. But if this really was his sight talking to him, then presumably it would tell him when he went the wrong way or if he was going to miss the mark. So he turned to the left, slow as a tortoise as he placed one foot in front of the other, never abandoning his slow, shuffling gait. By his calculations, he should have hit the tiled wall. He didn't. Did that mean he'd actually stepped inside a mirror, as the voice had suggested? He had no way of knowing—until he did.

The universe rippled, so quickly that it was almost imperceptible. He didn't even have time to flinch or break stride. One instant he was walking slowly across a grimy hospital room, and the next he was...somewhere else. And he could *see*.

It took him only an instant to recognize his surroundings. He was in the living room of a house. The air was warm and the house was quiet. There was a soft, old carpet under his feet, and the wallpaper looked like it had been there for decades. Sunlight entered the room through a window behind him, and he felt the merest hint of a breeze wafting through it. Looking down, he saw that he was a child again, in green pajamas with a blue trim. He was sitting in a brown chair in front of an old TV, a gigantic brown box with a rounded picture screen. No pictures ever appeared, only static. His father could only fall asleep with the static on, so he left it tuned to a dead channel all the time. Simon was very familiar with the soft whoosh of static waves, but no television programs.

His father wasn't there right now. He worked all week, and then sometimes over the weekends as a sad clown at other people's parties. By the time he got home, Simon's mother would be asleep; she said that looking after Simon was like having seven jobs and left her exhausted. Simon was the one who waited in the family room every night to hear the front door open and his father say in his regular dog-tired voice, "I'm freakin' home!"

His father came in, said hello, and hugged Simon tightly. Wrapped in the comfort of his father's loving arms, Simon opened his eyes as wide as possible, drinking in every detail, however large or small—from the colors of the walls, to the view through the windows, to the family photos on the table and the painting of his father as a clown that hung in the entry hall.

The return of his vision brought a rush of emotion like nothing he'd ever felt before, a joy that was not only new to him, but also seemed entirely new to the world: something born within him that he could now share with others. His father gave him a slice of cake he'd brought home from a birthday party he'd performed at, and Simon started to sing softly to himself through mouthfuls of sweet cake.

Then everything went dark again, as though someone had slammed a coffin lid shut over the scene.

"Ah! Wasn't that lovely!"

Simon was back in the hospital, or the prison, or whatever it really was. At any rate, he stood in the same room he'd been in before—he could feel the rough concrete floor and smell the ammonia in the air. Someone was standing in front of him, examining him. He heard a pen scratching on paper, and he smelled a faint tincture of perfume, so he knew it was probably a nurse. The mask was cutting into his face again, and his sight was talking to him in his head.

"Your father has a warm and delicious voice," his sight said. "Now, you can probably paint a picture of what part of your life this middle mirror will take you to. You were just there. Go on, and have fun!"

He did as he was told, shuffling and sliding toward the mirror as slowly as before. He felt once more the rippling effect, although it was perhaps more notice-able this time since he was expecting it.

Instead of his childhood home, Simon found himself in a park. The grass was a shade of green so bright it could have come from a bucket of paint, and the sky was full of clouds as white and fluffy as the wads of cotton lining the inside of bottles of pills. It was as if all the clouds were his best friends—not just friends, but a family, him and them together. He wasn't even shocked to be able to see them, not this time. He was expecting that, too.

He knew this park. He and his daughter Jane had sat here for hours, talking and simply enjoying being with each other. He could hear birds in the trees, and out of the corner of his eye he saw a rabbit emerge from a tangle of bushes, glance around, then return to its hiding place.

He had not thought of his daughter in a long time. Simon pictured her as an adult now, with a face almost identical to her mother's: Jenna. Everyone always said how much Jane looked like Jenna.

Simon kept calm as he looked at Jane. The moment in his childhood home had shattered abruptly and he didn't want this one to disappear the same way. Perhaps, if he remained perfectly still and absorbed as many details as possible, it would last longer. And, if it didn't, maybe it would at least feel that way.

To Simon, Jane had the beauty of a fairy tale princess. She had long black hair and wore no makeup. Her all black attire was visible underneath a green army coat that was really too heavy for the spring day, but she seemed perfectly comfortable. She was smiling at Simon. A tear slid down his cheek. *The sight of beauty is an open doorway, a portal to treasures we may not always recognize.*

"You look beautiful today, Jane." An asinine thing to say to the daughter you haven't seen in what feels like forever, but Simon felt barely able to speak as it was.

Jenna had died during childbirth and Jane, missing half of her heart, had been educated in a private school, saw a therapist every Tuesday, and attended a special hospital for those at risk for self-harm and suicide. Simon had worked two jobs to make ends meet. He didn't enjoy either of them, and neither paid well. He'd constant worried, and there was the occasional crisis—and yet, he and Jane had been happy overall.

"I had a great day at school today," Jane said. Her voice, which he thought was pitched a little high for a sixteen-year-old, made Simon still think of her as a little girl.

"Tell me?" Already, fully immersed in the moment and the conversation with the daughter he loved, Simon was starting to forget that none of this was real, that he would soon be back in the hospital.

"My best friend came back from seeing family. And they got me a gift!" Jane pulled a small, clear plastic bag from one of her coat pockets. Inside, a sparkly blue hamsa keychain caught the sunlight.

"That's wonderful, sweetheart," said Simon. He knew how something as small as a keychain could make a person happier than anything else in the world.

And then it was over. It had lasted a little longer than the visit to his childhood, but this time something pressed on his mouth, his cuts had begun to bleed once more, and all was dark. The room felt colder than it had before, but that could have been his body comparing it to the warm sunshine in the park.

His sight spoke to him again. "Such a lovely daughter you have, and what a trip this has been! This is the last one, I promise. Then, after we finish our main course, I've got something special for you. A surprise!"

A surprise? Well, he wasn't going to get too excited about that. They weren't going to give him back his sight; why bring him to this hospital in the first place if they were just going to reverse what they had done? Thoughts of surprises were a distraction, and he didn't doubt that that had been the voice's intention. He needed to stay focused and hold onto the happiness he'd felt in the park with Jane. In his memory, she still smiled at him; beneath the mask, he smiled a little, too.

"Step into the last mirror; don't be shy. You know nothing about it, buddy, but you'll get used to it. Promise." Simon walked slowly, shuffling step by step, toward the final mirror.

He was in the kind of restaurant he'd never ordinarily think to enter: dim lighting, no music, tables far enough apart that you couldn't overhear conversations, and waitstaff who seemed happy to be serving people.

He was wearing a suit. On the other side of the table was a woman he didn't remember ever seeing before. She was very beautiful, but surprisingly old. Did that mean he'd remarried? He looked at his hands; they were as dry and wrinkled as a turtle's feet, so he was much older, too. A cake with pink icing sat on the table between them, and in the center of the confection was a single white candle.

"Are you ready to make a wish, darling?" The woman's voice was soft, and he could hear the love in it. If he knew who she was, he was sure he would feel the same love for her. He smiled and blew out the candle. "I can't believe it's our first anniversary."

That settled his doubts about who she was and what they were doing together, but since they seemed to be in their late eighties and had been married for only a year, Simon was left with more questions than had been answered.

"You know something, Simon?" his new wife said. "No one visits us anymore. We never see your daughter or your grandchildren. Or anyone, really. We're just two people in a nursing home who never get any visitors. Does that bother you?"

Did it? It took a little thought, but he was fairly sure it didn't. The odd thing about these visits through the mirrors was that each new scenario was so different, but one thing was constant. He was always happy, and so was whoever he found there with him. He smiled, wondering about this woman. How had they met? How had they fallen in love? Something that struck him was the sheer size of his new wife's bag, like something one would bring if one were going to the beach for months.

Then, in the middle of cutting the cake for the anniversary of a wedding and a marriage he knew nothing about, he heard, "Alright, I'm sick of this! Time's up!"

This voice wasn't in his head this time. It was definitely coming from outside of his mind. Everything went black again, but this time he felt better prepared for it and was not shocked.

"Now that you're back, Simon, my people and I have a gift for you, all wrapped up with a big red bow," his sight-voice said. "Your gift is a choice, but you have to pick one way or the other—"

Simon yelped with involuntary joy, interrupting the sight-voice. He thought he knew where this was going, could feel his happiness glowing inside his chest like a diamond spinning in the light.

"Alright, alright, you germ. I'll tell you." Simon's sight-voice paused for dramatic effect again. "You must choose which life you want to live in, Simon: your past with your father, your present with your daughter, or the future with your new wife. I can say that I know you missed having a wife, Simon."

A choice? Not sight? Simon's mind felt like it was speeding down a highway with sudden stops and sharp turns. He growled, trying to speak though he couldn't find his words.

"You don't have a lot of time. Pick one!" his sight-voice shouted.

I loved being a kid, but I loved taking care of my daughter. But, I never thought I would fall in love again. To hear his father's singing, or to be with his sparkling daughter, or to live with a new wife and love again— these were his options.

How could he make a decision like that? Simon was in shock now, thinking it all had to be some kind of horrible dream. His mind was spinning in circles. Singing, sparkles, or new love. Sparkles or new singing, sparkles or new singing, sparkles or new! He began to scream behind his mask. The glowing diamond of happiness in his chest was turning red, cracking and smoking as it transformed into a jewel of rage. He bashed his head against one of the mirrors, screaming like a child.

"Oh, *that's* why your mother felt like she had seven jobs. Then your child had problems, all caused by you, and your new wife takes pills." His sight-voice sighed. "I'm tired of this. Time's up!"

What followed were three of the most horrific scenes Simon could imagine. First his father, hanging from the ceiling in Simon's childhood home, his hands struggling to free himself from the rope coiled tightly around his neck. Simon's scream was so high-pitched that it shattered a glass vase beside him. Next, his daughter lay dead on the grass in the park, her head missing. He hugged her, sobbing with rage as his tears mixed with Jane's blood. Then there was the smell of smoke and the same oppressive heat he'd have felt if he stood before an open oven. This was the restaurant where he and his new wife had been celebrating their anniversary, but she was not in her seat. The police and fire department were there, and Simon was watching from across the street, through a window. A cop spread yellow tape across the entrance.

Covered bodies lay on the sidewalk. It could have been weirdly restful, but Simon was filled with tension. He wanted them to be alive, and yet he wanted to see them die. To see burned skin. To see pain. When he pulled away the white blanket on one of the bodies, he saw his new wife, burned to death. They had shown him his whole life in less than ten minutes—then they'd shown him this. *This* was the great surprise.

He threw back his head and screamed so fiercely he was sure he'd wiped out his vocal cords.

Everything was white. He was back in the hospital room, but now he could actually see it. His eyes were where they should be, in his sockets. He still wore the pajamas, but there was no mask over his mouth and he held the handcuffs in his right hand.

"I'm not what I said I was," said the voice. "I'm not your sight. I'm not part of you. You are angry at the people who put you through this experience, and I'm one of them. When you were kidnapped, I was there. When the others played with you, so did I. You think this is a hospital? Maybe it is. But you were not brought here to be cured—quite the opposite. And since you're about to break down..." The voice paused. "You see the two nurses?" Simon looked and saw one on his left, one on his right. A man and a woman. They wore purple surgical masks with matching scrubs. "Patient J1518: kill! Kill them with your anger!"

The rage that surged through him freed him—freed him from the restraints of civilization. When he stabbed the male nurse in the throat with the end of the open handcuffs, setting free a jet of blood that doused Simon's own face and painted it red, the male nurse did not even flinch. It was as though he'd expected to die. The female nurse was smiling, but her death was not enough to satisfy his fury. He tore open her body with both the handcuffs and his hands, tearing at flesh and bones to find the heart, which he held, still beating, in his hands like a newborn child. He stood up, growling and barking like an animal. The door to the room was open and unguarded like an invitation to flee.

Still holding the woman's heart in his hand, Simon dropped the handcuffs and walked toward the door.

Q & D

A new setting made Quincy's eyes water. Where was he? He knew the place, and yet he couldn't quite place it. His head was swirling, as though he'd stood up too fast after lying down for a long time. Still dizzy, he looked up and all around, trying to orient himself.

And then he knew exactly where he was. This was the house they—he and his brother—grew up in. It was the only environment they knew before they got too old to be cared for. Or, too *much* to be cared for.

Sensory impressions washed over Quincy, memories attached to sights and sounds and smells. And yet, he saw it from a strange, slightly skewed angle that allowed him to notice every flaw. He couldn't remember how a single one of those broken windows ended up that way. The dried paint on the walls cracked and peeled away in strips, like the hide of the world's oldest alligator.

Having once been a church, the house still had a faded mark on the wall where a huge cross once hung, but the rows of benches were gone, leaving only a cavernous room whose tall windows let in enough light to stream across the floor in vertical strips. For twelve years, Quincy and his brother lived there, though not by choice. If you'd asked him, Quincy would have said it still looked like a chapel. But what did he know? He'd never been to a church that was actually being used as a church. What went on there? What did people do in churches, and why did they go there? He wasn't completely clueless; he could put together in his mind pictures of people singing. Shaking hands. Being given bread. But these images all came from movies and things he'd seen on TV.

When he and his brother lived here, it was surrounded by other buildings. Not any more. Now it stood on its own, a single tooth left in a jawbone in which everything else had rotted. Everything else seemed the same. The sky was gray and as opaque as a coat of paint, just as it had always been, and the dirt beneath his feet was black and dry as toast crumbs, just as it had always been. And yet, it wasn't.

Initially, coming back to his childhood home put him at ease. But that was draining away. The house, the desolate grounds... His gut spasmed, his mouth was dry, and he could hear his own heart beating so fast that he feared it would burst out of his body. He began to scream.

As a boy, Quincy was never alone. Daniel had always been there, or someone else. But Quincy had no recollection of solitude. And that was fine, because solitude was like death and being with others made Quincy more alive.

Even in the bathroom, he wasn't allowed to be alone. Daniel would be there. He'd face the corner, making it clear he wasn't looking, but every few seconds he'd say, "I'm right here." Sometimes the brothers had to eat the same thing out of the same plate or bowl. They even shared forks and knives.

Nor had there been any chance for solitude in a house that had once been a church and was surrounded by other buildings with people in them. But being hemmed in was good. Quincy liked hemmed in. Hemmed in meant never being alone. And now...

Quincy couldn't bear to look at this landscape of desolation any longer. This emptiness. This aloneness. He turned his attention to the ground, then crossed his arms to grip his shoulders and push his fingertips deep into the flesh near his neck, as though he was trying to trace his vertebrae—all in service of denying the sense that, if no one else was present, he couldn't be here, either. The more insistently he pushed, the more he felt the pressure in his whole body. This was what he'd wanted so often since he and Daniel left this place and went their separate ways: to push everything bad and fearful and disturbing out of himself.

Was it just TV and movies that told him what people did in church? He couldn't be sure, because what held him now was a deep, all-consuming spiritual hunger. A sense that he was empty and ready to be filled. And how could he know that if he'd never been in a place where spiritual hunger was catered to?

Daniel. He wanted Daniel: to find him, to run to him, to hug him. Connection. Affection. The fraternal bond. They were all there, inside him. He'd known them at some point. Memories were fickle, but the cells of your body, the acids and proteins that made you *you*—they didn't forget.

A ground floor window, one of the unbroken ones. The room was dark, but something had... Yes. There. The weak, flickering and fluttering flame of a small candle.

"Dan—"

Amazing that something as small as a lit candle could turn desolation and fear into hope and the attractions of home. He walked toward it as quickly as he could, his heart bouncing and thumping. Quincy loved his brother, and yet the feelings were those of a weak balloon animal. Something someone twisted into existence and that lasted for a while, but there were no illusions that it could be permanent. To the child who carried one into the circus, the balloon was a bonus, a little gift, something to make the child laugh, but never the main attraction.

He reached the front door of the house and turned the knob. He wanted to be able to shout loudly enough for Daniel to hear and come running from wherever he might have been. But all that came out of Quincy's mouth were the same small and strangled noises of a terrified dog: the sort of dog female Hollywood film stars might have carried in a bag.

And Daniel, in fact, didn't hear them at all. What he heard was the front door banging twice, pushing forward in its frame like someone or something was trying to force it open. Like an animal that wanted to get out of its cage.

Daniel was hiding in his favorite spot—right behind the kitchen counter, and two rooms from the front door, which was about as far as he could get from the outside world. Striving to be invisible, he crouched down with his arms wrapped around his torso, eyes shut tight, trying to catch his breath. He was already in the kitchen when he heard the noise, and immediately ducked out of sight. He didn't know who the visitor was, but whoever it was, Daniel wasn't about to welcome them. No one ever came to the house. Should he answer the door? Look out the window? Barricade every entrance? Maybe, just maybe, it was something innocent this time. It could be just the milkman. Or an old friend.

He shook his head violently. An old friend? They had no friends. It was probably an invasion. An attack launched by someone who hated and feared him. He already knew that people would scream and run away whenever they saw him or any member of his family. Now they had probably snapped and were going to come for him, for everyone.

Daniel knew that his mother and Quincy, the younger brother who needed his protection, were sleeping upstairs. Though, how anyone could still be sleeping after all this noise was beyond him.

Some boys seemed to have no difficulty transforming into men. It simply happened. They got taller, they grew hair where it had not grown before, their voices deepened. And, if they lived long enough, they became old men. A seamless passage from birth to the grave, and they all seemed to take it in stride. They knew what to expect, and knew that all was as it should be. They made enemies, sometimes, but mostly they made friends. Friends to ride bikes with, who became friends to double-date girls with, who became friends to drink beer with after a hard day at work.

It hadn't been that way for Daniel. In junior high, his best and only friend was his younger brother, Quincy. The two shared a room in their quiet, empty house. They slept in the same bed, sat in the same classrooms, and shared the same friends—though the friends never stayed true. They took meals together, even sharing food when there wasn't enough for two.

Quincy was Daniel's brother, and Daniel loved him, but there were still times when Daniel wanted to be alone. Sometimes he hid behind the kitchen counter, but Quincy knew he liked that spot and would always find him there. If Daniel wanted to truly be alone, he had only one choice: the piano. The control he got when he sat at the keys was total. He alone decided what to play. His hands decided which keys to strike, which mistakes would be made. He'd close his eyes, lay his fingers on the keys, and he was off on his own journey to the end of the street or the edge of the universe, and nothing and no one defined him but the sounds he created. At the piano, he could be the only man on Earth.

That had its attractions when the rest of the world was such a mystery. Their father had said he was going on a short business trip, but that was three months ago. Since then—nothing. No word, no contact, not even a letter in a bottle. It was pointless to ask his mother because she either killed the conversation with silence or said he'd be back "soon." Daniel had heard it said of other men who left their families that they were having an affair, and maybe that was what his father was doing. But what exactly was an affair? He had no idea. He knew it was a bad thing because of the way people spoke about it and, if his father was having one, Daniel thought he probably wouldn't want his father to come back. He knew, though, that that was not how his mother felt and decisions like that (all decisions, really) were made by adults and not by children. Given the results of those decisions, though, it was pretty obvious that adults weren't exactly qualified to make them, either.

And now they had a visitor, but it wasn't his father. His father would have shouted out his name and some kind of greeting, even though it was late and Daniel's mother and brother were asleep. That was just the kind of thing Daniel's father did. So Daniel hid in silence. His legs were starting to cramp from crouching for such a long time. His breathing grew labored, heavy and dry. His throat was so parched that he began making a hacking, wheezing noise as he inhaled and exhaled. It almost hurt to breathe, as if he had run a marathon, but he was perfectly still, frozen in place. He tasted sand on the roof of his mouth.

The banging at the front door stopped as it swung open, and someone—or something—was inside the house. Whoever or whatever was making noises, but they didn't sound like anything a human mouth would produce. They weren't words, but gasps and guttural cries—like a dog that had barked itself hoarse.

Daniel had to wake his mother. Surely she would know what to do. She was a mom, and moms knew everything. Right? Daniel stood slowly, memories of the last visitor flooding his mind. His ankle still hurt from that instance. Fully upright, he could still feel the rawness in his throat and the sandy dryness of his mouth. His ankle felt like it was wrapped in sharp metal.

Holding in every sound and pausing for a moment to think, Daniel ultimately ran for the stairs, fear at the forefront of his tangled mass of emotions. It seemed he banged into every piece of furniture they had along the way. How could one live in a house so crowded with pointless memories?

Struggling up the stairs took so much out of Daniel, he almost wouldn't have minded falling where he stood, unconscious and unaware of whatever happened next. But his fear of who or what was downstairs, grunting and gasping and invading his home, pushed him forward.

Two heavy dressers blocked the door to his mother's room, and he had to put his shoulder against them and slide them across the floor with loud screeches before he could turn the doorknob. The door swung open, and he heard music playing. There was a record on the turntable playing, an old song, the one his mother listened to every night to fall asleep. It was also Daniel's favorite song, but right now all he heard was the blood roaring in his ears and the sound of his heart pounding like a kettledrum.

He shook his mother's shoulder, yelling as loudly as he could. "Mother! Mother, please wake up!" He didn't even care if the invader—the monster, whatever it was downstairs—could hear him.

But she didn't move. Not one muscle in her body twitched. Daniel's mother always had the blanket pulled over her head when she slept. He grabbed it and yanked it backward, hoping the light and open air would awaken her.

The smell was appalling, like a burnt skillet full of dead flowers and broken twigs, covered with big red worms. And that was exactly how his mother—his dead mother—looked lying there in that bed.

Daniel clamped his hand over his mouth as he ran out from the room and toward his brother's. Before he could get there, though, sorrow and guilt washed over him. He fell to the wooden floor and started crying.

Nothing in his mother's life had been her fault. None of it. Yes, she had moved her children into an empty church, which she then filled with a seemingly endless parade of furniture. Yes, she had set fires, and yes, her husband had disappeared, but none of it was her fault. Maybe the fencing that could be found all over their house was there because she had seen it as a prison. That would explain why their clothes were stacked all the way to the ceiling, why there were dressers nailed into the walls and lamps, and rolled up rugs and chairs all over the floor. In a strange way, he was starting to feel like he understood his mother better than he ever had—perhaps because he had never thought from her perspective before. How often do children think about their parents' ideas, thoughts or feelings? Not often enough.

Burning random places down might have been an adult joke Daniel couldn't understand. Maybe by the time he was older, he would laugh and sing like his mother had when she burned down this building or that. No hard work, just play.

He was suddenly distracted by something dripping on his neck, back and shoulders, and the powerful smell of sea salt. He tried to ignore it and let the memories of his mother play over and over, but the dripping didn't stop.

Finally, he lifted his head. The smell of salt was so strong that it was as if he had snorted wet seaweed fresh from the ocean. It was physically repellent; he was gagging, choking to death on the scent alone. Daniel groaned and slowly stood up. "My God, what—"

From right behind him, a deep growl rumbled.

When Daniel looked over his shoulder, his heart froze. The sight of his mother, dead for heaven knew how long, was nothing compared to this monster. The skin on its twisted face was like the bark of a white oak tree, its layers peeling away and leaving a trail of bark-like skin all the way from the front door and up the stairs. Growths all over its body looked like snail shells. From a distance, though, they could have been little holes inflicted by something stabbing the creature over and over. It had an underbite, and its teeth were a deep, nutlike brown—like wood. Its seven eyes were all clumped so close together that Daniel wondered whether they could even focus properly.

One glance at this drooling creature and Daniel's brain screamed at him to get away, but it was too late; the monster grabbed him by his shoulder.

Daniel cried out, "I'm sorry, please!"

The monster gripped him in its massive limbs and lifted him off the ground. Daniel's whole body was on fire with the wish to be saved. If Daniel had been even capable of thought at that moment, he would have seen from the way the monster's mouth watered that it was hungry. Daniel fought helplessly. He felt the monster's mouth wrap around his entire neck, and then he knew no more. The monster swallowed it all— the pumping blood, his vocal cords—before crushing Daniel's head and throwing what was left of Daniel's body to the floor.

The monster began to shake and rumble and scream in pain. Its skin sloughed off in slow waves of melting bark. Fingers became visible. Its animalistic cries changed into the yells of a distraught human being. The protrusions on its skin burst, draining a greasy green liquid down its torso and limbs. The monster was dead, and Daniel's little brother, Quincy, lived in its place.

His breath was heavy in his lungs. Walking through the remnants of the dead monster's body scattered around his feet felt like stepping into a foaming white sea. Later, he might wonder why he wasn't surprised by this turn or events. What is certain is that the moment he returned to his human form, he remembered everything that had happened. Instead of being shocked that his brother was dead, it felt inevitable. It was something that had to happen, something for which he was prepared.

As such, Quincy knew he had only minutes to do what must be done if he was to avoid being alone forever. He picked up Daniel's remains and ran down the stairs. It only took him seconds to reach the basement, but felt like years. *This will work, Danny. I won't be alone.*

The heavy wooden table on which Quincy laid Daniel's body, like a butcher's board or a workbench, was one of the few items of furniture their mother had brought home that he actually found useful. He took the scissors from his pocket and cut into Daniel's chest. He pulled out Daniel's heart; it didn't need to beat anymore. Quincy stood still with the heart in his hand, then laid it down. He pulled out the machine and placed it right next to Daniel's heartless, mutilated body. He took from the machine's mouth the flask of clear blue liquid labeled: *For Brother*. The liquid's purpose was to raise the undead. The stories had better be true, or... He didn't want to think about the alternative. Daniel's essence had returned him from his monstrous fate, but if the liquid could not work a similar miracle on Daniel, Quincy would be alone forever. He poured the liquid into Daniel's mouth and waited. And waited. Nothing.

The machine quivered. From deep within it came a low growl. It twitched; its limbs began to move. Slowly at first, and then in fits and bursts resembling the movements of a baby suddenly emerging from sleep. It was still as its eyes opened. It stared at Quincy, at first with no sign of recognition. And then...

"Quincy," the machine said. "How long was I asleep?"

Quincy started crying with relief. He had his brother back.

WALKING MONSTER

I t was a perfect fit. There was just the right amount of space for Redmond to do what needed to be done. All he had to do was apply the right amount of pressure. The action itself was familiar, one he had performed many times before.

This was just one of Redmond's many established patterns. He spent all day in his room, and over time his life became all about repetitive actions that slowly, imperceptibly, transformed into rituals. It was not always this way; he had a real life before, but could not picture it now. One day he was doing something, the next it was just the way things were done, and then he couldn't imagine doing it any other way. Finally, he was convinced that if he ever changed the pattern, something terrible would happen.

That was how Redmond lived. He did things the same way every day because he knew—just *knew*—that if he didn't, the world would end. Somehow. The details were unclear, and he couldn't remember who had told him he had to do these things, but doom was certain if he didn't do his part.

But then there were times when he had to break his patterns. This was always terrifying, because if he was doing something for the first time, how did he know he was doing it right? Maybe he wasn't. Maybe something terrible would happen as a result of the thing he did, instead of because of something he didn't do—which was Redmond's other fear. He always had to make sure he did everything he had to do, every single day, so that bad things wouldn't happen. He had a list in his head that covered from the time he woke up to the time he went to sleep again, and all the tasks had to be done the right way and in the right order. Doing something before it was time to do it could be just as bad as not doing it at all, or doing it incorrectly. So he followed his list, item by item, making sure to perform each task perfectly, and always finished just in time to go to sleep, reassured that, because he had done everything he was supposed to do, the world had not ended, and he would have another chance to save it the next day.

The thing he was about to do was something he had done not once, but many times. It had never gone wrong. And yet as he prepared himself for action, his hands shook so badly he could barely hold on to the tool he needed. The rubber wrapping on its metal handles managed to be at the same time both sticky and slippery in his sweaty palm. He tightened his grip, but not so much that it would slide out of his grasp and land on the floor. If he dropped it, he would have to start all over again, according to proper procedure, and that would mean picking up the tool, cleaning it off, sitting back down on the chair again, placing his feet flat on the floor and at the correct distance apart... No, it was better to do it right the first time. He repeated in his head the words spoken to him so many years ago by someone he could no longer remember. *If you don't have time to do it right, how are you going to find time to do it again?*

He tightened his grip again and cleared his mind. He was ready. He was strong. He was focused. He would do what needed to be done. He had repeated the mantra more times than he could count and, even if he didn't really quite believe it, it hadn't failed him yet.

The perfect pressure of his grip turned into overwhelming strength. It was the special, different type of strength a person would work for weeks to conjure up, to nurture within themselves before letting it out and using it at the exact right moment. Moving his tool into position and squeezing it tightly in his still sweaty, yet cooler and not quite as slick, hand, Redmond began to pull.

The pain erupted instantly. Redmond didn't understand why it hurt, but it did. And why was his body so unwilling to follow orders? His brain knew that this was necessary, and his brain controlled the rest of him, so why was his body putting up a fight? Why did it ache, and feel as though it was being stretched to the point of snapping, like taffy stored in the freezer? And then there was the fear that if he pulled any harder, disaster would strike. His muscles began to tighten; his own body was actively fighting him. Part of him knew what had to be done and wanted to do it as quickly and efficiently as possible, but another part of him was resisting, fearful and trying to keep things the way they were. It was a battle that Redmond could not lose.

But losing it he was. He was going to have to force his body to cooperate. He held his breath like a sailor who had fallen overboard, feeling the chill of death all around. Redmond thought about the task he had to perform, and told himself that he would not let his body show weakness. He would not let it shirk its responsibilities.

With all the strength he had, he gripped the tool and pulled as hard as he could. He felt that frozen-taffy stretching feeling again, from deep inside, as though something attached to the inside of his heel was being yanked all the way up his body and out of his mouth. He began to sweat—not just his on hands, but everywhere, all over his body. His shirt grew damp and then wet, and a trickle of perspiration ran down his temple from his hairline. He began to feel as though he was murdering himself, but he knew he just had to push through. When the last small part refused to let go, he pulled harder until it finally surrendered to its fate.

Redmond had prevailed. He had pulled it out. He held up his tooth, which was secure in the tool's grip. He could feel blood filling his mouth. When he swallowed it, it was warm.

Redmond leaned forward and dropped his tool and the tooth to the floor. He rested his hands on his knees, breathing slowly in and out through his nose. If he breathed through his mouth, the hole where the tooth had been would pulse uncomfortably, like he had pressed an ice cube to it. Exhaustion suddenly pushed him to the edge of consciousness. He thought he might pass out, sliding right out of the chair to the floor. He wiped the sweat off his forehead. His shirt was cooling, sticking to his back, and he shivered slightly. He tried to keep himself aware by focusing on the throbbing of the nerve that had once been attached to his tooth. He looked down at it, lying there on the floor, white and pink. His mouth hurt so much he was almost certain that he would see flesh attached to it, torn from his jaw, but it was small and white and clean except for a tiny stain of blood. He stared at it in a kind of fascinated horror, unable to believe it had come out of him even though he was the person who had pulled it free. Maybe he could put it back? He reached for it, then stopped himself. No, it was meant to be pulled out. This was one of his tasks. He had to perform them, correctly and in the right order, and he could not undo or redo anything. What was done was done.

Finally, Redmond stood up and walked to the far side of the room. This was unscheduled activity—he had more things to do—but at least for the moment, his curiosity was stronger than his sense of duty. He looked at himself in the small, smudged mirror that hung over the sink where he brushed his teeth twice a day. One less tooth to brush now, he thought, a laugh freezing in his throat. His brown hair hung over his forehead, almost covering his eyes. He swiped at it with one hand, pushing it away. His dark gray eyes looked like asphalt dried in the hot sun and, to him at least, seemed to be too close together, pinching on either side of his big, flat nose. He didn't remember ever breaking his nose, but it sure looked like it had been, and more than once at that. Sometimes he snored so loudly through his crooked nose that he woke himself up. He opened his mouth to see what it looked like in there, without one of his back teeth. His jaw hurt from stretching it all the way open, but he leaned back so the light could penetrate the dark cavern of his mouth and show him what he wanted to see. He couldn't quite pick out the hole by sight, but he could still feel it.

Air flowed into his mouth again, touching the exposed wound and giving him chills. He reached into his mouth with one grubby, calloused finger and carefully touched the open gum. The pain was already receding, but was that really so? Was his blood still dripping? He pulled his finger out of his mouth and looked at it—no blood on the tip. That was good. The gum throbbed slightly. Every time his heart beat, it seemed like the gum swelled, then receded.

Was this how he was supposed to feel, or was there something wrong with him? He had done what he was told to do, so the pain and the fear must have been part of that. But why? Why would it be his mission—his duty—to make himself feel bad? Why should he always do what he was told, if it was going to feel this way? Was this really his entire purpose in life?

Yes, of course, you idiot, the voice thundered in his brain. It was so loud that he almost expected to see every object in the room shake, but nothing happened.

The voice was inside him, like a vibration in his bones. His whole skull rattled and bounced when the voice spoke to him, turning his mind into a madhouse. He tried to give the voice what it wanted, but it was never satisfied.

Do what you're told! Do what you're told, you walking monster! You traitor! You are an unwanted pet! Look at you in your own slaughterhouse!

In a way, Redmond didn't mind these words. He knew the voice cared about him, or it wouldn't go to the trouble to say such things. He knew what he did was important. If it wasn't, he wouldn't have received such strict orders about what was to be done and how he was supposed to do it. He wouldn't have been warned so starkly about the consequences if he didn't follow through. Or had he been told? He thought he had, but maybe he was...wrong? Maybe his habits had somehow become compulsions? Had he done this to himself? He shook his head. No, that couldn't be it. He had a mission, and missions did not appear out of nowhere. They were given, assigned. They mattered.

His mental spiral of anxiety was broken when some undefinable impulse made him look to his left. He scanned his room, but everything was the same. Still, he was unsettled. The room no longer felt like his space, as though something in the air was filtering into his mind and body, corrupting his senses and warping his perceptions. From where he stood by the mirror, the brown and comfortable chair in which he had spent so many hours—the very chair he'd been sitting in when he had pulled his tooth—no longer looked familiar to him. Redmond felt like an outcast, an interloper. Had he really sat in that chair? He couldn't be sure anymore.

He looked at the window—or rather, he looked at the opposite wall and saw that there was a window. Windows did not simply appear, so he supposed it must always have been there. But that was logic speaking, not memory. He looked again. The blinds were shut tight, keeping almost all the daylight out, but they were hanging poorly and needed adjustment. If they'd always been there, why wouldn't he have noticed before now?

Just go over there.

Of all the many commands he'd received from the voice, this one affected him the most. Stepping forward meant having to step forward again, and if he backed up then he would have to start all over again. But deep inside he felt the seeds of change taking root; parts of him began to want to question what they were told to do. Like the tooth that had not wanted to come out, even though the rest of him worked to remove it. Finally, he walked slowly, thoughtfully back to his seat. As he got closer, he knew that this was in fact his chair, that he had sat there many times, that this was his room and he belonged here. That the window belonged, too. He didn't sit, though. He was back on the path; he had things to do.

His lips stung from breathing heavily through his mouth; the air still aggravated his wound in a way that made him flinch. He shut his mouth and began breathing through his nose slowly and deliberately. He walked all the way across the room, away from the chair and over to the window. As he got closer, the blinds looked worse. They were dirty and shut tight, so that almost no light came through the cracks. He grabbed the handle and slowly turned it with two fingers, watching the slats open up and the light filter through, first in slivers and then all at once. He could see every individual speck of dust on the blinds. They were awful. He thought that he should clean them, but there was no response from the voice. Cleaning the blinds was not one of his jobs, apparently.

Did he even still fit the story this room had to tell? Was he really still the person for those jobs the voice had given him?

Before picking up his binoculars, Redmond took a deep breath. He forgot to use his nose, and opened his mouth wide, sucking in so much air he thought he felt his jaw crack. The force of it probed at his injured gum like a sharp fingernail, stabbing all the way up to the top of his skull. His chest expanded till he thought his ribs might pop. What would happen if he accidentally swallowed all that air? Would he puff up like a balloon? He thought he had better force it back out again and wrapped his arms around his torso, then exhaled as hard as he could with a massive *whoosh*. The air left his body in a long, slow push, and for an instant he felt like an empty bag on a closet shelf. Then he felt light-headed, as though all the blood had drained out of his body. Without thinking about it, he sucked in another deep breath, and the cycle resumed.

Frustration erupted within him, like a fireworks display of pure, futile rage. Why was he subject to these endless patterns? Wake up. Perform a task. Perform another. Perform another. Keep going all day, performing task after task until he was exhausted. Then sleep. When he woke up, it began again, and all without encouragement or praise or reward. But if he missed one task or was even slightly in the wrong, the criticism and abuse were relentless. This was his life. Task after task, with no end goal and no indication that the cycle would ever end. Seven days a week, every second of every hour. He wondered that sometimes – what would be the consequences of failure, or of abandoning his responsibilities completely. What if he just...stopped?

Shut up. You will do your job. You will never stop, you worthless creature.

It was so loud, so angry, so forceful. Pain shot through his head as though someone had lit a fire inside his brain. Tears leaked from his eyes and down his cheeks. He stumbled back and away from the window, his eyes half-closed, and almost fell over before he bumped into the chair and caught himself. The chair. His chair. He caressed the rough leather, which was warm in the sunlight through the window, like the skin of a pet elephant. Using his hand as a guide, he moved around the chair and slowly sank into it. He sat there for a moment, recovering from the wrath of the voice. When he felt better, he stood up again. Now he was behind schedule for sure. This day was not going the way he wanted it to. He had so much to do, and so little time.

Redmond walked back to the window, slowly and carefully, as though the floor itself might suddenly attack him. When he got there, he picked up his binoculars and leaned toward the blinds, carefully pushing the lens between two of the slats. Looking through the binoculars, he saw what he expected to. The world outside was so bright, so much brighter than his room. He winced, but did not let himself close his eyes again. It was his job to look, to see.

The road beneath his window was long and straight. Redmond turned his head to one side and looked as far into the distance as he could, until his eyes began to water and his vision grew blurry, but he could not see the end of the road. He turned his head and looked in the other direction, but saw nothing new. As far as he knew, he had never been on that road. He had been in this room for as long as he could remember. Perhaps he would be there forever, staring out at the road like a dog waiting for its master to come home from work.

A building on the other side of the road seemed somehow familiar, though. It was a hospital; he didn't know how he knew that, but he did. Maybe he had been inside it once. He pictured a dark room with tiles on every wall and a dirty floor. But if he had always been here, how could he have been there? How could he know what a room in that hospital looked like? He waited, braced, for the voice to shout at him for thinking about this, but it didn't.

The long, straight road was always the same. It never changed. But was that right? It seemed to Redmond that it *was* changing. Eventually it would reach its breaking point and something would happen. Perhaps that was what he was supposed to be watching for. Perhaps he had to warn everyone when the road became dangerous in some way.

The road and the cars were all part of one living system, Redmond thought. It was their habitat. He wasn't sure where he'd learned that word, but somehow he knew it was the right one. Mother Nature's gifts stood all around, flanking the sides of the road. Tall trees with the most stunning green leaves adorning their broad branches flowed into the trunk like veins and seemed to reach out, scooping up the air and bringing it toward themselves for harvest. The wood practically cried out to Redmond; even through the glass of the window he felt as though he could smell the life force throbbing within the trees. It gave him a rush of pleasure. He knew that the chair and the floor and the window frame and even the walls of the room he was in were made of wood, but none of them had the life force in them—not anymore. Caressing the leg of the chair would not bring him that kind of joy, the feeling of communing with another living thing that he thought he would feel if he could just go down and touch one of those trees. He wanted to feel its rough bark under his palm, or climb onto one of its branches and feel it flex beneath his weight.

But he had to stay in the room. He had work to do.

He stopped for a moment to gaze out the window. Gray smoke filled the sky as clouds and plumes erupted from the earth, billowing upwards and drifting past the sun until they blocked the light and floated away to be replaced by another wave. Bombs had exploded for days on end, sending great waves of dirt into the sky and turning buildings into rubble. Now there was a victory, and a celebration, but who won, what the prize was, and why it was something to be celebrated—all these things were beyond Redmond.

The road had somehow remained untouched, and the cars stayed in constant motion, traveling to a destination Redmond couldn't identify. They never seemed to stop coming or going. And all the while, he stayed inside his room, doing what he was told had to be done. He did not listen when people below cried out in pain and fear, or called for help. He stayed inside, like a child who had been locked in a closet while the adults did "grown-up" things. But now it was calmer out there. The explosions had stopped, and so had the screaming. Only the smoke remained, and the movements of people and cars on the road below.

Redmond looked through the binoculars at the road again, trying to focus on individual vehicles. If he didn't pay close enough attention, they became a blur, like a thousand versions of the same car endlessly passing by, so he made the extra effort. He tried to look at each car as it passed, and study as many details about it as he could before it vanished out of sight. Did it have two doors or four? Did it have only a driver, or were there passengers, too? Could he tell by looking at people's faces where they were going? He didn't think he could, but he tried anyway. That man was smiling, so he was probably not going to work. That woman looked angry and drove fast; someone was in the passenger seat. Maybe she was going to meet someone who owed her money.

He couldn't remember the last time he'd talked to another person. He watched from his window, because that was what the voice told him to do, but he never got to ask them what they were doing, where they were going or why, to find out if his intuition was ever right. Car after car passed, and to Redmond each one was a potential encounter gone forever. A deep sadness engulfed him when he considered that here they were, all in the same world, the same reality, but somehow they could never connect.

Suddenly Redmond realized something that he had never noticed before, and when he did, it was the only thing he could focus on. All the cars were the same color: bright, shiny red. Their fenders caught the sunlight and set gleaming explosions of light off the chrome of their bumpers and hubcaps and the big wings on the end, in the back. What were they called? He knew the word. He put the binoculars down and thought about it. It had something to do with fish. He paced in a circle, one step after the next, trying not to disturb anything, and as he walked he wiggled his hips slightly, as if he were swimming. What was the name? Fins. That was it. Tailfins. He smiled; now he could move on. He picked the binoculars up again, and returned his gaze to the road. One red car after another. But wait—what was this?

He could not be seeing what he was seeing. He closed his eyes, holding them shut for a long moment, until he almost began to enjoy the darkness. Then he opened them again and looked through the binoculars. It was still there; it must have been real. He took a deep breath, a breath that no longer hurt his mouth, and slowly let it out. He looked out the window at the road, at the two straight lines of cars that sat there. Traffic was frozen in place. The cars' engines were running, but not one moved forward, or even back, so much as an inch. The drivers could have turned their cars' motors off, gotten out, and laid down on the street without any harm coming to them.

Redmond looked closely and paid attention to every detail. He had to look—this was the reason he was here, in this place. This was one of his jobs now. He moved the binoculars slowly across the window, scanning from left to right, examining each car as carefully as possible before moving on to the next. Now that the cars were standing still, this was a little easier. The sunlight gleamed off the metal, though it was still filtered by the smoke in the distance, turning the air slightly gray. He kept the window shut tight so that the smoke wouldn't come inside and make his eyes water. He needed to see clearly.

His hands began to shake and he nearly dropped the binoculars when he spotted the first boy. He was huddled in the back seat of a four-door red car, almost on the floor. Redmond could see one of his feet through the side window, and glimpsed his face through the back window. The boy trembled and looked up every few seconds, glancing around like a rabbit scanning the horizon for predators. Redmond could almost see the boy's nose twitching, sniffing the air.

The boy shifted position suddenly, startling Redmond. He pressed his face up to the window and looked around. For an instant, Redmond could have sworn that the boy saw him. His eyes seemed to light up, and then, he waved one hand. It was a small, barely noticeable gesture, and he looked as though just the action of waving left him petrified with fear. As soon as it was done he slid back down, obviously worried that the man driving the car might have seen him. But in those few seconds, Redmond had seen everything there was to see. The boy had been beaten, that much was obvious—beaten so hard and so often he was probably used to the sound of his skull cracking.

His skin was burned, his nails had been torn off from what he could tell, and most importantly, it looked as though his teeth had been pulled out—not all of them, but many. This was the way the boy's caretaker liked it. This was what brought him pleasure.

All these caretakers played games of lust, exploring the good and bad places of their captive children's bodies. They created pleasure for themselves, grateful for every moment they spent with their little brats bleeding and crying. The boy Redmond saw had felt it all, that much was obvious. He was near his breaking point, feeling not just that the end of his life might come any moment, but that he might in many ways welcome it. Redmond could see him crying harder and harder as he lay there in the car. His body convulsed with sorrow and fear and desperation. His mouth was open and Redmond could tell that he was wailing out loud, but the man at the wheel of the motionless car did not turn around or even seem to pay any attention at all to what was going on behind him. He just didn't care.

Redmond turned away and looked at the next car. There was another little boy in its back seat, abused and beaten, his teeth and nails torn away just like the one in the car behind him. It was an endless cycle. Every morning, hundreds of cars passed by Redmond's window, leaving the city, dropping these wounded children off in some mysterious place Redmond had never seen, knew nothing about, and would never visit. Part of him wondered why these caretakers would want to just throw away their property this way, but that line of thinking was what always caused the voice to scream at him, so he stopped. He just did his job.

The realization, when it came, was like a safe inside his brain suddenly cracking open, the door flying wide and all the contents exploding out all over the room. He *did* know where those children were going. He had been there himself.

Redmond had been one of those boys. He had been taken to the brick building far out on the edge of town, and brought down into the dark basement, and had stood under the single cold white light in the ceiling to watch as another boy came out of the darkness on the other side of the room. When the bell rang, he had charged forward and punched that other boy in the face and the ribs and the stomach as hard and as fast as he could. The other boy fell over, and if he'd tried to get up Redmond would hit him again and again—whatever it took to win. That was how Redmond's family got enough money to stay in their home and eat for another month. He had kept fighting, and winning, for years, until he got too old and started slowing down and losing. That was when his face had gotten smashed in, and they'd put him in this room and given him a new job.

It all came washing over him like a wave, and he fell to the floor, hugging his knees and shaking as the memories filled his brain.

Some time later, Redmond heard a massive crash behind him, so loud and sudden that he panicked and dropped the binoculars as he leaped to his feet, looking around. The wooden doorframe to his apartment splintered as a man wearing heavy boots kicked the door in. He stomped into the room like a giant, and two other men dressed in dark blue overalls followed. The first man, the one who had kicked in Redmond's door, was bald with a head the size of a pumpkin and a bright red face. The other two had skin the color of black coffee. They stood together, staring at Redmond, before the red-faced man stepped forward, grabbed him by his shirt, and threw him to the floor. His bones rattled as they hit the hard wood, like an unused piano that someone had opened for the first time in years and played, all the keys striking in a harsh cacophony of sound. The red-faced man took Redmond's binoculars, smiling appreciatively as he hung them around his own neck. One of the two dark-skinned men bent over, grabbed Redmond by the elbow, and dragged him upright.

Redmond was too frightened to even defend himself. Why had the voice not told him this would happen? Who were these men? Didn't they know he was here for a reason? Didn't they know he had work to do? His mouth hurt again.

The red-faced man stood directly in front of Redmond. His breath was foul, and there were deep bags under his bloodshot eyes. When he smiled, it was one of the most frightening things Redmond had ever seen, revealing teeth as yellow as split wood chips. The man grabbed Redmond's face in one gigantic hand and forced his mouth open with the other. His filthy fingers tasted like dirt and undercooked meat. Redmond gagged. The man pushed his mouth open all the way, staring into it. He saw the missing tooth and smirked. "The waves still rage on," he said.

What that meant, Redmond had no idea, but with the man's fingers stuffed into his mouth he couldn't respond even if he'd wanted to. Why were they here? Why wasn't the voice protecting him, or telling him what to say? He had work to do. He was falling behind schedule. Panic built in his chest—the schedule was all.

And then, the other two men began smashing everything in the room. They started with his chair, lifting it up in the air and slamming it to the floor so that the legs flew off the frame. Then they attacked his bed. When the red-faced man let go of him and walked over to what remained of the desk, Redmond stood where he was, unable to move. He watched, mute, as the man picked up his flat cap and bag and dropped them on the ground. What was he to do? How was he to defend himself, to save himself and his possessions?

Suddenly, the two men each grabbed one of his arms and dragged him from the room. Someone else passed him, going in the opposite direction: a young man, clean cut, dressed all in black, and looking both relieved and excited to see the now vacant room. Redmond looked over his shoulder, back into the space that had so recently been his. The new man was consulting with the three men in coveralls. They were giving his room to someone else. And fruit—they were offering him fresh fruit! Redmond could not remember the last time he'd had fresh fruit. Certainly no one had ever given it to him for free.

And what the devil was this? People were coming out of other rooms on the same floor to welcome their new neighbor—people completely unknown to Redmond. Not one of them had ever talked to him. Not that he'd have wanted them to; they would only have gotten in the way of his work. He hadn't even known there were so many rooms on this floor, or in this building. No, he wouldn't have welcomed their social advances, but that didn't mean he had to like it when they pushed past him like he wasn't even there, like he was just an obstacle to maneuver around. One of the men came out into the hallway and changed Redmond's room number. It had been 4M, but now it was 1M. He did it without a word, but looked at Redmond as if to ask why he was still there.

Redmond walked down the hallway. Every room that had been numbered 4 was now numbered 1. The walls were painted a deep, throbbing red. *This must be how it felt to be inside a heart.*

But never mind that; this was also how it felt to have one's very identity taken away. He had had a fixed idea of who and what he was, but his eviction had taken that idea and tossed it on the scrapheap. If he didn't live in that room, if he didn't do what he had always been expected to do, what was he? Would the world end now? And where was the voice? The voice was always there, warning him, helping him, advising him—until now.

One of the other doors was open. Inside, a violinist was playing along with a classical record. He didn't look up as Redmond passed, so Redmond didn't stop to listen. He didn't know anything about music anyway, so he wouldn't feel comfortable telling the man he played well. Honestly, he could have played atrociously, and apart from the fact that Redmond didn't want to lie, didn't like lying, if the man thought Redmond was patronizing him he might not react well.

When he reached the lobby, the woman at the front desk typing on her typewriter. A stack of novels sat next to her. They were stories of inspiring people doing amazing things—gods and their perfect lives. It seemed to Redmond that the woman's typing was gaining speed as she possibly worked on another adventure, creating her own myths of perfect goddesses. Although what she was actually typing, Redmond had no idea.

He could see the door leading out of the building. The sun was bright and he should have wanted to get out there and feel it—for the first time in so long—on his pale skin. But he didn't. What he wanted instead was to run back upstairs and throw all those people out of his room. It was his. He needed to be there. There was work to be done. He had already spent so much time saving the planet from evil by doing his job, day after day, waking and working and sleeping and waking and working and sleeping... But now what? No one cared that he had been there, no one cared that he was leaving, and he was damn certain that no one cared about what he was going to do next, or even if he survived.

But there simply wasn't a choice. He couldn't go back, so he exited the building and gingerly stepped onto the grass lining the side of the road. Every stride was like a nail driven into his flesh. He wanted to run back, but he knew he couldn't. So, where could he go?

Smoke wafted through the air. The gleaming red cars were moving again. He looked at them from close up this time—not through his binoculars. They seemed bigger, stronger, with fenders bulging like dinosaurs' muscles that seemed to flex as they pushed their way down the road, engines growling angrily. Each one carried a terrified child with a toothless mouth open wide in a scream as its owner gazed at Redmond as if he could help.

Redmond didn't want to think about them anymore. He wanted to get away, to leave this world entirely. But he didn't know where to go. He was safe in his room. Where else would he be safe? And then it came to him: Boomer. His friend Boomer would help him, if he could get to him, and he'd be safe. Redmond looked around, remembering how the streets were laid out and where they led. He could get to Boomer from here. As he walked, he avoided all contact and looked at nothing but his shoes.

Would people think he was crazy? Of course not—they'd think he was a man on a mission. A man with a place to go to and someone to see.

And they'd be right.

GLASS

4 8, 49, 50. There were 50 tiles on the left wall of Sarah's small bathroom. She sat on the floor counting them while her clothes dried. She had counted them hundreds of times; she could even tell the individual tiles apart. The second tile in the third row had a tiny chip in its top left corner. The fifth tile in the second row had a small teardrop-shaped streak of something—maybe putty or caulk—permanently adhered to its surface. She had picked and picked at it with her nails, and even licked it to see if it could be softened up, but it never changed. It was tiny, but solid. It would never go away.

Her clothes were still drying. Sarah began counting the tiles on the right wall. There were more of them, even though the two walls seemed like they were the same height and width. It was a puzzle she could never quite figure out. She counted in reverse this time. 60, 59, 58...

Tomorrow was going to be "look at the floor for the first half of the day, then the ceiling the next half" day.

Sarah wrapped herself in one of the few towels she had. It was damp, and smelled vile, but the others were worse. Several of them lay in a coiled heap in the corner, like the nest of some cantankerous animal. There were spots, especially near the corners, where the fabric was almost see-through. She wrapped it tightly around herself anyway; there was a light breeze flowing through the room, though she couldn't identify its source. The walls all seemed solid, with no holes or cracks. Even the door was wedged tight against the frame; when she ran the hot water, the air barely circulated and the room filled with steam. So where was the breeze coming from? She supposed it didn't matter. What mattered was that it was there.

She curled up into a tight ball, the damp towel providing very little protection, but was still somehow better than nothing. Sarah finished counting the tiles, but the accomplishment held no pleasure or thrill. It felt like a board game she played every night, to the point that she'd completely committed the board to memory—she could see it with her eyes closed, and the second she rolled the dice she already knew what square she was going to land on. Ultimately, all the enjoyment had long since drained out of the experience, until it was like running on a treadmill. She'd all but lost the will to play and, in the end, she'd have rather just called it a day.

Her clothes dripped, and tiny drops of water hit the floor, playing a soft melody that sang to her of gradual but perceptible progress. Other people felt anger toward their enemies. Other people sometimes felt hotheaded or bitter. But that was other people, not Sarah. Sarah accepted her life and lived moment by moment. Counting tiles. Waiting for clothes to dry. Hours passed this way each day, so many that she lost count. In the end, she always found herself wearing the same dress she'd worn a thousand times before. But Sarah didn't mind.

Her clothes were comfortable; they had the softness of long wear and the almost blurry appearance of garments that had seen years of hard work. Looking at them brought memories of better days, of where she'd been, what she'd done there, and how good it had felt at the time. She might have been in a small room where the sun never shone, where the weak, cold breeze had a mysterious origin, and where the only light came from a fluorescent tube above her head. But once upon a time, the sun had warmed her clothes and the wind had blown them around. She could still bring those happy times to mind.

The fluorescent tube hummed and sometimes flickered from behind its wire cage. Sometimes there was a thump at the door, and voices outside in the hallway asked to be let in, but Sarah never opened the door or even acknowledged them anymore. The voices called, some more than others, but even the most persistent eventually stopped and went away. Occasionally, she heard footsteps pass by without any attempts to communicate with her at all. Part of her was happy about that—it was an acknowledgement that she was there for a reason—but another small part of her wanted to be wanted. It was one thing to refuse people entry; it was quite another to feel that no one wanted to join her in the first place. Still, the clothes held fond memories, and the hope that comfort and relaxation might one day be hers again. The gentle fabric slid over her skin like a caressing hand.

All these thoughts pleased her, but they could not take away the cold of the damp room. Moisture came through the thin towel, raising goosebumps all over her skin and causing her to shiver uncontrollably. At last, she decided that she was simply too busy to continue to lie on the floor, wrapped in her towel and wallowing in her discomfort. So, she pulled the dull, overused dress over her head and wriggled into its embrace. Her spirits rose instantaneously. Somehow, she felt warmer and more sheltered. It was no paradise, she wouldn't fool herself that much, but it was something. When she looked down at the dress, she didn't see it as it really was, the patterns faded almost to uniform grayness. Sarah saw the bright colors that, at one time, everyone else would have, but with a rich tint and glow added just for her by the memories the garment carried, which were woven into its fabric as tightly as any thread.

Once she was fully clothed again, she knelt down on the floor and leaned her elbows on the rim of the pink bathtub. A slow smile spread across her face, until the room almost seemed brighter than it had been mere moments earlier. Her oddly charming friends swam around slowly.

Before taking up residence in the bathroom, she had never realized how beautiful a turtle's seemingly gloomy colors could be. There were dozens of them in the water, paddling around in circles, their dark eyes and stubby snouts and silence conveying a strange kind of intelligence. Some were the size of a coin, others that of a saucer, but none seemed to be in charge or taking care of any of the others. Male or female, they were equally cute, and all part of one collective turtle kingdom. They didn't even have names, because she couldn't keep track of them long enough to assign any. They moved slowly, though not as slowly as she would have expected, but they never stopped. They bumped into each other, swiveling their small stublike heads around to see if there was a way to steal food from one another. Even then, they held a gentle, dignified air that Sarah thought in turtle language must mean, "Oh, excuse me, and have a nice day."

She looked up and all around the room, scanning each wall from the uppermost corners of the ceiling to where they met the floor. She had to stop herself from counting the tiles again. *You already did that.*

The feeling that crept over her like a warm bath made her feel welcome. Though what it was that welcomed her, she could not have said. One by one, she turned her attention to every single thing in the room and thanked it for being there for her and with her. The walls, the sink, the tiles, even the tiny smear of whatever-it-was on the tile. She was grateful for its presence, as she was grateful for everything in the room, from her threadbare towel to her old faded dress to every turtle, from the smallest to the largest of the bunch. She wanted all these things to know just how grateful she was, because who knows which bathroom they'd be in next? She might never have another moment with them.

Thank you, thank you, thank you. At first, the words were spoken only in her head. But then, as her emotions grew stronger, she began to whisper them and then speak them out loud at full volume. Eventually, she shouted the words at the ceiling, like she was calling on the universe. Her spirit responded by filling her entire body. She wrapped her arms around herself—not because she was cold, but because she was suddenly aware of the overflow within her, until she could imagine it bursting through her skin and out into the world. She stood and spun in circles, feeling that at any moment her feet would leave the ground and she would rise up to the clouds before sliding back down on the smooth arc of a rainbow.

Slowly descending from her fantasy, she sat down in her usual spot again, looking down into the tub where the turtles swam. Like a persistent household pet, Sarah's hunger helped her measure the hours of the day. At the moment she was not starving or famished, but she could definitely feel the need for food building, like a kind of desperation. But her own needs would have to wait.

Sarah stood up and took the little cardboard box down from its shelf, halfway up the wall in the corner above the toilet. She would feed her turtles first. The healthier they were, the better their lives would be. Looking at them every day as she did, Sarah sometimes felt that she gave them more than she should, treated them too well, pampered them, but she couldn't stop herself. Their snub-nosed faces and impassive black eyes somehow spoke to her. Watching their tiny flippers wave as they swam through the water in the bathtub, occasionally colliding peacefully with each other, calmed her.

She worked hard to make the bathroom feel as much like a home for them as she could. One day, though, she knew they would crawl out of the bright pink bathroom, leaving the light brown, stagnant water of the bathtub behind so they could live in a big open pond in the woods. They would swim as far as they wanted, eat leaves that fell from the trees overlooking their new home, and interact with all the other creatures in the great big world: ducks, squirrels, fish. It would be a good life.

She opened the box and shook flakes of food onto the surface of the water. She moved her arm back and forth over the tub, making sure it didn't clump up in one spot. She didn't want them all crowding together, fighting for food; she wanted them to relax and eat in comfort.

They weren't at all relaxed, of course. The turtles swam around each spot where the food landed, sucking it into their tiny beaks with quick gulps. She wondered if they even took pleasure in it. Did it taste good to them? They closed their eyes when they opened their beaks to eat it, but was that a sign of enjoyment, or just a reflex? Their heads and shells bumped together as they kicked their flippers to stay above the water and swallow as many of the tiny brown and orange flakes as they could. Some food became waterlogged and sank to the bottom of the tub, as it always did. None of the turtles chased it. They ignored it as it drifted down and formed a new layer on top of those already present at the bottom. It was like sediment, sitting there and occasionally shifting a bit if frantic turtle movements created small currents in the water.

When the rest of the food was all gone, the turtles went their separate ways once more. The bigger ones headed for the corners of the tub, while a few of the smaller ones gathered into groups and swam together, as though they meant to protect themselves against some danger only they could perceive. That's when it was time for Sarah to eat just enough of her own food to keep her energy up. She sat and pulled her knees up to her chest, wrapping her arms around them and rocking slightly from side to side.

Sounds of discomfort and disapproval seemed to be coming from above, but when she looked up, she saw nothing. They might have been in her head—that had happened before—but this time she didn't think so. She didn't like hearing disapproval, at least not directed at her, and it was even worse when it came from that seemingly disconnected perspective. Guilt rose up and filled the room, making her world seem smaller and smaller, and suddenly, with a force that made her shrink into the floor, it hit her that she had done a terrible thing.

She burst into tears. Her face grew hot as salty tears ran down her face. She toppled over and crawled across the floor and back again on her knees, howling out her guilt. She screamed desperate apologies in a hoarse and agonized voice, apologies to her real friend. Her surroundings proved that someone else knew what was best for her. This was where she deserved to be, where she needed to be, until her crimes were forgiven. She would stay and count the tiles, wrap herself in a thin towel, and wash her clothes until all her sins were washed away with the dirt. Until she was clean.

Punishment was now her friend. If one betrays another, the best way to make amends was to feel their pain just as acutely. They had to feel the proper degree of shame for what they had done, no matter how much time it took. Sarah knew why she was in the bathroom, and her shame made her feel even colder as she sat alone in the room, the turtles her only companions. She wrapped her arms tightly around herself again and squeezed, hoping to get warm, but it was no use. Her knees began to ache where they rubbed against the cold, hard tiles, the skin scraping. They hadn't yet started to bleed, but it wouldn't be long.

She reached into the tub and wet the fingers of her right hand. A few turtles swam toward her, bumping against her as though trying to decide whether she was food or another animal. They lost all interest and swam away when they realized she was neither.

She rubbed at her knees with the water from the tub. Her allies were trying to overpower her guilt, to make her feel unjustly imprisoned. Their emotions radiated in her direction like waves of heat, each more intense than the one before.

She knew the bathroom itself did not take her seriously. It took everything she could throw at it and remained impassive. She shouted at the walls, scraped at the tiles with her nails, thumped the door with her fists, kicked her feet in the tub and splashed the water all over the floor. None of it mattered, none of it changed anything. And somehow that didn't trouble her. Her inability to change anything served only to relax her. To her, the room was a shelter, not a prison.

But in reality, the room was not benevolent. It wasn't even neutral. She could think of it however she liked, but the bathroom didn't care. She could try to reach out, to connect, to make it her home—or at any rate, a place that could be in any way welcoming—but there was never any response. In fact, there were times when it seemed almost cruel. It grew stronger and stronger, and every time it lashed out at her, its power increased while hers diminished, to the point that she was weaker than she had been when she first arrived. Not that she could remember when that was, though, judging by the state of her clothes, she had been there a long time.

She stopped screaming and closed her mouth with a soft *pop*. Her cheekbones felt cold and numb. She caressed them with her fingers, moving the skin up and down in slow circles. She dropped her hands to her sides, touching the floor, exploring its stillness. The temperature in the room was steadily dropping. She felt it first in her teeth and gums before it spread to her jawbone and the rest of her head, like frost forming on her brain. And from there, the cold streamed through her body, filling her veins like ice water, turning her muscles hard and brittle, and cooling her blood even as it passed through her heart. She felt so, so cold.

This was what she got. Punishment was all that mattered in life, and this was hers. A force of air came out of nowhere and pushed her back. The cold crushed her body like ice, crackling and rumbling as she slid all the way to the tiles, where the damp towel lay within reach but provided no comfort. She was surrounded by eyes, thousands of judging eyes. She apologized yet again to the room, to the universe.

She lay there for what felt like an hour before her energy began to return and she was able to prop herself up on her elbows. Warmth returned slowly to her body, and tears flowed down her cheeks. It had felt so awful when the cold surged through her; she had no idea what caused it, but she knew she never wanted to feel that way again.

Something was crawling on her face. Not tears, as she would have expected, but something totally separate from her skittering across her skin. And yet, her searching fingertips found nothing. Whatever was there knew how to evade her touch. She gave up on being subtle and wiped her face hard, then harder still, and then her entire hand rubbed more and more vigorously, faster and faster, like someone desperately trying to start a fire by rubbing two sticks together. Rubbing turned into scratching, yet the tickling sensation persisted. And still, she could not dislodge whatever caused it.

"Get off me!" The scream came from deep inside her and she screamed over and over, her howls of fear and agitation echoing off the tiles. "Get off me, get off me, get off me! Off me! Off me! Me! Me! Me!"

Standing up took more effort than she might have thought herself capable of, and yet, she propelled herself off the ground and then gripped the edge of the bathtub, shoving herself upright with such force that the air whooshed out of her lungs. She had to pause, inhaling deeply while she came back to herself. She looked down into the water. The turtles seemed to have heard the commotion; several had swum in her direction, and one or two even seemed to be looking right at her. She didn't fool herself into thinking that they were worried about her. They probably hoped the noise and her sudden appearance meant more food for them.

When her legs quivered, she only had time to wonder whether they would continue to support her when, without warning, they didn't. Sarah caught herself when she fell, bracing herself once more on the edge of the tub. This time, the turtles paid her less attention. So much for friendship. These creatures that she cared for saw her as a source of food. No more than that. Was everything she thought she knew false? The motivations that she imagined the turtles had, those that she thought the person keeping her imprisoned here had—were they all false?

She pushed herself upright, willing feeling back to her legs and strengthen her posture. She started swinging her arms back and forth and around her body, as if she were doing calisthenics. She swung them harder and harder, faster and faster, feeling the blood flow throughout her body with more vigor. She had been cold; now she was sweating.

Sarah stretched her arms out right in front of her face, then spread them wide, as wide as the distance between herself and her humanity. Though there was no one in the room with her, she was suddenly convinced that she felt two hands gripping her wrists. They were big, rough hands, like those of a lumberjack or a factory worker. They scraped her skin, cutting off her freedom. She stepped backward, slowly and carefully, until her back and shoulders touched the far wall.

A saying occurred to her, something she believed she had heard or read in the past. "If you don't like your life, you can change it."

Ha! Easy enough for someone else to say. But she did stop screaming. She smiled. She even laughed as her fear and tension and discomfort all faded away. The wall, sturdy and strong, held her up. She laughed as she imagined there being no door at all anymore, only walls. She told herself that the bathroom would never let her go. She rolled her shoulders in slow circles, rubbing her back against the tiles and laughing harder and harder at her pain—physical and emotional. Her laughter became uncontrollable; the bathtub was the funniest joke in the world.

Sarah related to the tub as she would to a friend who sat right next to her but never said a word. They had nothing in common, yet their relationship seemed to grow stronger over time. She had so much she wanted to tell it, and so she did, babbling until she was going on about absolutely nothing, though she couldn't be certain that the words ever really got around her laughter.

Slowly, she stopped laughing and eventually went completely still. Drowsiness returned, the same drowsiness that had been her natural way of life since some time after she arrived here. Sent here. No, call it what it was: imprisoned here. It felt like her soul leaving her body, seeping out of her bit by bit like steam leaking from a microwaved meal. But was there such a thing as a soul? Well, she had one, and right now it resembled a hot air balloon, lifting up and away, helping her persevere within the confinement that was her life. All she had to do was float free and she could journey beyond the stars. She closed her eyes and imagined herself drifting through the endless nothingness of space, passing a black hole, observing comets and swirling galaxies immeasurable distances away, all floating in the blackness just like her. Earlier, she thought she knew peace, but never in her life had she felt *this* peaceful. She rubbed her shoulders against the tiles again and found the way they grazed her skin to be intensely soothing.

The day was coming to an end. She slid to the floor and tried to sleep, to dream of space, but each time unconsciousness started to descend like a soft cotton blanket dropped from above, she felt a pinch on her ear or heard a soft whisper telling her what a good life she had and jolted awake. And then she was back in the bathroom, aware of everything around her.

At last, she knew what she needed to do. She crawled to the lip of the tub and looked at the turtles swimming in their slow circles. None seemed even slightly interested in her. She reached into the water and picked up one of the smallest ones. It flapped its tiny legs in the air, but when she held it in her hand, it pulled all its limbs inside its shell; only the tip of its snout remained visible. When she poked the tip of its beak with a fingertip, it retreated even further.

"Fine," she said. "Be that way." She lowered it to the floor with great care, setting it down by the door. She picked up another, this one about the size of a hamburger, and held it in her hand, too. This one was braver. It kicked its feet like it was still swimming, and stared directly at her. When she pointed a finger at it, it opened its beak like it meant to eat her and emitted a tiny croaking hiss. She put it on the floor next to the smaller one, which shifted slightly and huddled next to its larger neighbor for shelter.

One by one, she transferred all of the turtles from the water to the floor, where, as their numbers increased, they took up more and more space and she found herself sliding sideways along the edge of the tube to avoid stepping on them. Eventually, she had to stack the tiniest ones on the biggest ones' backs. None of them seemed to mind.

When all the turtles were out of the tub, she opened the bathroom door for the first time.

"Out you go," she said.

One or two of them looked back at her, but none moved. Finally, she reached out for one of the biggest ones and, as gently as she could, pinched the tip of its tail. It twitched slightly and took a slow step forward, then another. Soon, it was out the door and in the hallway. Another smaller turtle followed it, and another followed that one, and so on for about fifteen minutes until every single turtle had decided that it, too, ought to go.

For the first time in as long as she could remember, Sarah was alone. She let out a deep, exhausted breath and felt a deep sense of relief, along with something much more important. There wasn't anything keeping her there. The room's power was gone. She was free to leave. She stood up slowly and brushed herself off, opened the bathroom door, then paused, looking all around the room, waiting to see what would happen next. Could it really be that simple?

When nothing at all happened, she stepped across the threshold and paused again. All the turtles were gone—she had no idea where, but the carpet was slightly damp where they'd crawled away on their clawed feet.

Apart from her, the house seemed empty. She walked downstairs and opened the front door to find that everything outside was beautiful. The sun was high in the sky, the grass was green, and the air was warm and welcoming. But the instant she crossed the threshold, there was a loud and horrifying crack, as though a massive axe had split a sheet of plywood in the sky. Even as she cringed, wondering if she should return to the bathroom or take her chances out there, something even more startling happened. What seemed like an infinite number of glass shards, some as tiny as a fingernail and some large as icicles or stalactites, fell from the sky. Some crash-landed flat, some stabbed into the ground, and others shattered upon impact until the surrounding area was covered in sharp glass fragments. And then the shower of glass simply stopped.

She looked around, waiting for something else to happen. The glass crunched beneath her feet, but did not cut her bare feet. Still, she walked slowly and carefully to the street.

People were coming out of other houses now, looking around, assessing the damage. They gathered in small groups, talking, consulting one another. Some of them saw her and whispered with their hands over their mouths, as if they were afraid that she would overhear them. Then one woman pushed a nearby man's shoulder, shoving him toward Sarah. He stumbled in her direction and stopped just in front of her, his face a mask of nervous tension.

She smiled at him and said, "Hi."

"Why... Why are you outside?" he asked.

Well, why was she? But, more importantly, why shouldn't she be? She smiled, but didn't answer. Then she looked over his shoulder at the woman who had pushed him toward her. Her face was a mask of fury.

"You did this!" she shouted at Sarah, waving one arm in a wide circle as if to indicate the entire world. "If you had stayed inside, this wouldn't have happened! Now what will happen?"

Sarah smiled even more broadly. "I don't know. Isn't it exciting?" She stepped around the man and continued down the street, enjoying the warm sun on her face. No one else said a word.

THE COLD ROOM

Boomer, head nurse at Brookville Memorial Hospital, listened to the pounding on his office door. He recognized the voice shouting his name; it belonged to Redmond. Boomer knew that he was one of the very few people Redmond thought of as a friend. For all he knew, he was the *only* person Redmond thought of as a friend.

Did he see Redmond in the same way? He wasn't sure. Neither of them was a native of this country, and that did bring them close in an odd sort of way. But close enough to be friends? Perhaps.

What was clear was that Redmond needed help, and he wasn't going away until he got it.

"Boomer, you have to help!" shouted Redmond.

Redmond spent most of his time alone; he was, Boomer supposed, unused to talking. While they weren't from the same part of the world, they both got similar stares from Brookville natives and, whenever they approached anyone, heard the same grumbles of, "I hope he speaks English." Actually, Redmond didn't hear that, because no one talked to him at all; they shrank away from him as though he were dangerous. So, different though their lives were different, they were both "them" to the people who considered themselves to be "us," and that created a sort of bond between them.

The blue liquid Boomer was chugging was so cold it gave him brain freeze. Holding it in one hand, he opened the door with the other, then wiped his mouth and threw the empty bottle away. Packing a bag of NACL supplies and his own medicine, he said, "Give me two seconds."

"We don't have two seconds," shouted Redmond. He was always in a state of panic, always convinced that whatever he was doing was the most important thing in the world. Be that as it may, Boomer could tell but this time something more serious was going on.

The second he left his office, Redmond turned on his heel and they made it down the hall in almost no time at all.

"Redmond, what's going on?"

"I got thrown out. They threw me out of my place. They let someone else in there."

"You're kidding! How is that possible? How did—"

"I have no idea what's going on," Redmond said, flapping one giant hand at Boomer like he was shooing away a fly. "No one told me a damn thing. What am I to do now? My job is helping people. Protecting people. I need to protect the children, but they're trying to stop me. They threw me out." He suddenly looked around. "You can see it."

"See what?"

"Pain," said Redmond. "The patients' pain. It drifts out of their rooms. It fills this corridor like a dark yellow fog. You see it, right?"

Boomer shook his head. Clearly, Redmond had a problem and thought that he, Boomer, could help solve it. But how was he to do that if the man couldn't even keep his mind on task? "I'm sorry, I don't see anything."

"It's like ammonia vapors. Let it fill your nose and it will burn you. It's from these poor devils in your charge. They'd rather surrender than recover, would rather be blown away to hell than have what's left of the rest of their lives restored."

Boomer said, "With the greatest respect, you don't know what you're talking about. I deal with these people every day and—"

"They would," Redmond insisted. "Because at least death offers certainty. No one wants to live in one big enigma."

Boomer decided to ignore that unsavory comment on his life's work. As they headed further down the hall, he said, "You'd think you would've had some kind of idea that something was wrong."

It was an attempt to get Redmond out of his own

head so he could focus on the matter at hand. Boomer put up with Redmond's madness because, most of the time, it was harmless and the guy could actually be nice. This seemed worse than his usual rambling, though. He was doing more dancing around the subject than anything else. But, he also looked genuinely scared, which made Boomer feel even more nervous. He just had to wait until they got wherever his friend was leading him to figure out just how bad the situation was, and what kind of solution they might pursue.

"We have to help the children," Redmond suddenly said.

Boomer didn't know exactly what he meant by this, though he'd heard his friend talk in the past about his own horrible youth, when he'd had to fight other boys for food and sometimes money. It sounded terrible, but Boomer was still a little annoyed by Redmond when he got so needy. He told Boomer he was trying to save people, but it always seemed like Redmond was the one who needed saving, and Boomer was more than a little tired of being the one to do it.

Redmond's wide eyes seemed to absorb everything around him. His mind may not have always been in control, but he was always taking in information and always seemed to find a path that led him straight to a crisis. The problem with that was that Boomer always seemed to be following him and ended up dealing with it, too. They passed the doctors' common rooms and offices, and headed for the first of the patients' rooms.

Boomer was accustomed to relative quiet in this

hallway, with no sounds other than the beeping machines and the nurses' soft footfalls moving from room to room, checking on their patients as they slept and healed. But today was different. Today it sounded like they were in a field hospital in the middle of a war. Screams erupted from every room, and moans of agony and fear cut through the air like a butcher's knife through beef. Even worse were the sounds of flesh being scraped, ripped and torn—of fingernails dragging down a limb, with skin and flesh peeling away. It was awful. The perpetrator—someone he couldn't see, and didn't want to see—let out a low groan, as if out of both pain and pleasure at the same time. Boomer shuddered and looked down at the floor, attempting to focus on the dirty white tiles and the intricate patterns created by thousands of shoes scuffing and kicking past day after day for years. If he focused on that, the sounds seemed to get softer and more muffled, and he was less anxious despite the patients' turmoil.

He'd always been a little jealous of how comfortable and clean the patients' beds looked. The sheets were always clean and white, unlike the gray rags and ragged blanket he slept under in his apartment on those few occasions he could even get home after pulling one long shift after another. No one would believe how perfect and clean this hospital was. The floor and walls shone like a magic mirror in which one might see a cleaner, better version in one's reflection.

Boomer stopped in his tracks. He needed to calm himself down, so he did what he always worked; he turned and looked at the wall, standing perfectly still like a punished child. Pausing for a moment like this allowed him to ask himself if he was on the right path, if he was genuinely being a good person. He thought about this all the time. Why had he taken a job centered on helping other people? Did he really care about them? Or did he just want their gratitude?

He thought about how he felt when a patient left the hospital. Was he glad, knowing that they were going home to their family? Or did he only care if they thanked him on the way out? And were those good feelings enough to outweigh the bad ones? He had to admit that he hated the sight of blood, and the smell of it even more. Sometimes people who were badly injured, or in enough pain, pissed and shit themselves. Cleaning it up was the worst part of the job. He had to stop himself from seeing the same old disturbing and disgusting messes every day. If he let it get inside his brain, he wound up feeling bad for everyone: the patients, the doctors, the nurses, even the janitors. When he felt that start to happen, he would turn away and stare at the wall until his mind went blank, smoothing out like snow falling on the surface of a frozen pond. It didn't usually last very long. Today it dissipated almost instantly, drowned out by screams of agony.

A nurse was trying to stop a young boy from scratching his leg so hard was getting more and more frustrated. Without hesitation, Redmond stepped forward to offer his help. Boomer tagged along like a little kid on a leash, though he was the one who should have intervened. The nurse was trying to put restraints on the patient, but it wasn't going well; they were having a wrestling match over the matter. The patient was small and thin, but fear lent him incredible strength. His arms and legs flailed in all directions, tossing the nurse around as though she were his teddy bear. Redmond waded into the battle and secured the restraints on the right side while the nurse fumbled with the ones on the left. When Boomer looked into Redmond's eyes, he could see that the man was wounded by the boy's pain, though almost no emotion appeared on his face. He eventually managed to tighten the straps, immobilizing the frantic, panicked kid.

Redmond looked at Boomer standing by and asked, "Are you going to tighten the other side one or not?"

Holding down the right side had him fully occupied and the nurse was rapidly losing control of her end. Boomer was familiar with the mechanics of the restraints, but he went very slowly, lest the kid to attack him, too. He grabbed the boy's wrist and felt fear coursing through it like electricity through a power cable. When he yanked his arm away, Boomer reached out to grab it again; the boy's wild expression and bulging eyes rolling around his skull made him hesitate. Redmond noticed, and made an impatient face as he leaned over and tightened the other restraint himself. Boomer stepped back, embarrassed that he'd dropped the ball on something so simple.

His limbs immobilized, the patient screamed. "So itchy!" he sobbed. His desperate need to relieve the discomfort by clawing away his skin was practically tangible. Boomer could not drag his eyes from the sores covering the patient's body—some open and weeping, and so red it was difficult to believe they were real. What could cause the body to react like this?

"Thank you. Everyone else has been so busy," the nurse said with a relieved sigh. Her uniform and haircut matched the pristine cleanliness surrounding her. She had the same kind of calmness that the doctors had. The nurse thanked them both again, which made Boomer feel bad because he hadn't really done anything. Redmond started to walk away, unable to meet the nurse's eye, and Boomer dutifully followed him.

The nurses and doctors were all trying anything they could to stop the patients from clawing at their wounds, or creating new ones. A doctor on Boomer's right side passed out at the sight of a patient ripping and tearing at her own gums with her nails until her teeth began to wiggle and then come loose, followed by gushes of blood. Boomer envied the man; he was free, if only for a while, from the screams and the agony of the scene. A child all the way down the hall on the left reached into her socket and scratched at her eyeball until it burst open, leaking blood and a weird clear fluid down her face in a slick river. It wasn't her first injury; scars all over her body gave the impression of a child who seen too much of what the world could give.

Boomer forced himself to keep walking, following Redmond to the end of the long hallway while patients ripped and tore at their bodies everywhere he looked. Despite the horror of it all, something made him want to look. And he couldn't stop himself even though he wanted to close his eyes and run straight into the nearest wall, to stare into the blank whiteness until his mind was empty and clear. But there was no time for that. He just had to try not to see the pools of blood, the missing hands and legs and lips and teeth. Never having experienced it himself, Boomer couldn't relate to the trauma of losing part of a person's body, but he understood the pain that came when a part of your life had been taken away.

Finally, they reached the end of the hall. A sign by the door read EXIT FORM 1. Another sign below it read ENTER FORM 2.

"Thank you for your help back there," Boomer said to Redmond. "You really helped that boy. Now that he's restrained, they'll be able to help him."

"That's all I want," Redmond said. "I want to help the children. I want to save them."

"Save them from what?" Boomer asked.

"They're being destroyed," Redmond replied, and looked Boomer right in the eye with an expression that made his friend shudder. "They take them away in the red cars and they make them fight, or sometimes they kill them outright. I used to watch out for them, but then they threw me out of my room. I don't think they want anybody looking out for them anymore. They want to be totally free to do whatever they want without anyone interfering. But I'm going to stop them. I *have* to stop them. And you have to help. You have to help me, Boomer."

"But what can I do? I have to stay and help these children here."

Redmond's face fell as he collapsed into himself; at Boomer's resistance, when one of his only friends in the world was reluctant to lend a hand, he likely felt that his mission was a failure. He folded his arms around himself and began shuffling his feet, shivering. Boomer knew that look, and he had to do something to keep his friend from spiraling into self-destruction. But what?

They entered a small room between hallways, which separated the one they'd just left from the rest of the hospital. Boomer felt like an astronaut getting ready to leap out into airless space. This cold room was at the heart of the hospital. They used it for confidential procedures, operations that might cost people more than their lives—things went on in that cold room that added trauma to patients' souls, and sometimes to doctors' as well. The cold was not just external. Once inside the room, it felt as though frost crystals formed on one's heart and brain. Boomer hated going in there, but suddenly he had an idea.

"I think I know someone here who could really use your help."

"I don't know," Redmond said without looking up. Boomer had expected this response. Redmond often put on a mask to cover his fear or shame or sorrow.

Boomer wondered whether he was about to do the

right thing. But of course he was. His friend needed a mission. He felt ineffectual and useless, especially when there was so much work to be done. Getting a grip on himself, Boomer stepped up to the panel beside the door and entered a long sequence of numbers he could scarcely believe he had memorized. The door to the cold room popped open with a hiss, and Boomer felt the frozen air blast him right in the face. He didn't care for the cold at all. If it were up to him, he'd spend every day of his life on the beach, under the blazing sun. He was already shivering as he led Redmond into the cold room, its icy blue fluorescent lights humming like the vibration of the heart of the universe.

In the center of the room stood a little girl. She couldn't be more than six years old. Her long, wavy hair was parted in the middle and fell over her shoulders; she was very pale, with dark eyes the color of ripe blue-berries, and she was totally calm as she watched them approach. She wore a thin hospital gown, the same as all the other patients, and she was barefoot. Boomer couldn't see the rest of her body, but her face and arms were covered in scars as thick as ropes. Some looked old, as though they were inflicted upon her years ago. Others were still red and newly puckered.

The cold pierced the thick-soled sneakers Boomer wore, so he had no idea how she was withstanding the temperature. She wasn't even shivering.

"Hello?" he said. Redmond hadn't said anything; he simply stared at the little girl like someone stuck in a dream.

"Hello, Boomer," said the little girl. "Hello, Redmond."

Boomer couldn't tell if she had spoken out loud, or if he had heard her voice in his mind; he was too pre-occupied to check and make sure her lips were moving. Then again, if she greeted him in his mind, she would have done the same for Redmond in *his* mind. He didn't suppose he would have heard that, too.

"This is Martha," Boomer told Redmond.

"Martha," Redmond repeated slowly, almost as if he didn't think anybody named little girls Martha anymore. It was a bit uncommon, Boomer supposed. "Why are you in here, Martha?"

"Because I like the cold. When I'm cold it doesn't hurt."

"What hurts?"

"Everything. That's why I hurt other people."

"You hurt other people? How?"

"With my brain. I picture them hurting, and then they do. That's why they pull their skin off and stuff. I told them to. If I hurt, I want them to hurt."

"But they're in a lot of pain," Boomer said. "Some of them will even die because they're so badly injured."

Martha's face crumpled as a single tear dropped from her blueberry-colored eye. "I'm sorry."

"Do you really feel better in here?"

She nodded. Another tear fell, and Martha cried harder as Boomer turned to Redmond and asked, "Can you help her?"

"Yes," Redmond said. He stepped forward and reached out to take her arm and lead her out of the cold room. He thought that maybe if he brought her out into the hospital and showed her how badly she was making the other children feel, she would stop.

"No!" she screamed. The force of her voice alone drove Redmond back toward the door, and Boomer watched in shock as he slammed into the door. The door clanged loudly, and Redmond slid down to the floor and sat there for a moment, breathing heavily.

Boomer stood very still and said nothing.

"Stay with me, Boomer," said Martha. "If you stay, I'll be good. If you leave, I'll hurt everyone—even you."

Boomer took one wary step forward. Martha's expression seemed friendly enough, despite her threats. He took another step forward. She looked the same. He was right in front of her as he looked down and folded his arms across his chest. It was extremely cold; the air was freezing him through his clothes.

"I can't stay in here with you, Martha," he finally said. "I have to go help the other children. But Redmond can stay with you. He can help you. Isn't that right, Redmond?"

He turned and looked over his shoulder just as Redmond stood up and brushed himself off. There wasn't any dust on his clothes; the cold room was very clean, so the motion was more reflex than anything. He nodded at Boomer and walked closer, slowly this time.

Martha looked at him, waiting for him to speak.

Instead, Redmond sat down directly in front of her. He then folded his hands in his lap and began to talk to her. He spoke softly as he told her all about his child-hood, about all the fights and all the pain and all the sadness and all the fear. He told her about the room he had lived in for so many years. He described how the voice had told him what to do and how he had thought he was being good, fulfilling his purpose, but then one day was thrown away like trash. He told her every-thing, and she sat silently, eyes wide, and listened.

When he was done, she moved closer to him and sat on his lap very carefully, as though she was wor-ried about tearing open some of her scars in the pro-cess. Then she wrapped her arms around his waist and pressed her head against his chest.

Boomer was happy. Redmond had Martha, and Martha had Redmond, and he could get back to work.

ON THE BOAT

"**K**eep rowing," Maria said. "Just a little farther, then we'll stop."

The boat moved slowly across the lake. The water was a deep, dark shade of green, and it was impossible to see through it. But every once in a while, a fish would rise to the surface, pop its small blunt face out as though it wanted to test the air, then disappear again. Maria swung her head from side to side, waiting to see when a fish would pop up next. She wanted to touch one, but they were always too far from the boat.

She had only ever touched a dead fish. That was terrible; its scales had come off as she ran her finger down the side of its body, and the flesh had felt like rubber, caving beneath her touch and then slowly reinflating as she lifted her finger away. And it had smelled awful. She wondered if a fish lifted straight

out of the water would have that thick odor reminis-
cent of cold soup. If she could ever catch a fish, she
would lift it straight up to her nose and find out. But
the fish stayed away from the boat. Maybe they were
lifting their little heads out of the water to see her,
to judge whether she was a threat or not. She wasn't,
but how could they know that? She couldn't tell them.
Was there even a fish language?

Rebecca stopped rowing, lifting the oars up into the
boat and laying them down along the bottom. Water
dripped from the flat blades, which didn't quite fit
and hung out over the stern. They continued drifting,
their momentum pushing them through the murky
water. Maria wondered how far they would go before
Rebecca would have to start rowing again.

Rebecca wiped her forehead, which was sweaty
from the exertion. "Next time, you row."

"Okay," Maria said, but didn't mean. They had been
friends since they were five years old, and their relationship had always been the same. Maria decided
where they were going to go, what they were going
to play, what kind of music they liked, what movies
they would see, and who else they were going to be
friends with. Rebecca agreed. When there was work
to be done, Maria made the plans and Rebecca did the
work. It was Maria's idea to row the boat out into the
lake, but both of them knew all along that Rebecca
would be the one rowing.

She didn't think, though, that Rebecca felt exploited
or abused. She knew her ideas were mostly good ones,

and she would allow herself to be talked out of things that Rebecca really didn't want to do. And Rebecca always seemed to have fun hanging out with her.

Today was a good day. The sun was bright and high in the sky. There were people on the shore of the lake, but there were no other boats near them. They had a vast area all to themselves. They could sit and talk and watch the fish pop up while the birds flew down and tried to grab the fish, and all was peaceful and calm.

And they could wear bright colors. They had been wearing black every day for what seemed like months, but today they could wear whatever they wanted. Rebecca's dress was bright yellow with a white collar and cut off just above her knees. Maria was wearing pink capri pants and a tangerine top.

"So why did you want to come out here?" Rebecca asked. They had left early in the morning, taking a long bus ride from the street they lived on to the center of town and then out again, heading for the park on the very edge of Brookville. In fact, the lake was one of the markers indicating the town's borders. Maria had heard there was a place there where they could be happy and young.

There were only old people on the bus: a few women going to factory jobs or to the hospital for their shifts, an old man in the back wearing old black clothes. He had missed a button on his shirt, leaving a small gap through which a patch of wrinkly skin almost as yellow as his teeth could be seen, and his cuffs were frayed. He kept reaching into his breast pocket, as if he was afraid that whatever was in there would disappear, and his lips and jaw moved convulsively, like he was chewing on a piece of caramel the size of a fist. His eyes bulged like a frog's, and he kept looking all around, examining everything and everyone else on the bus.

When Rebecca and Maria had gotten on, they looked at him for just a second. They were afraid that if they stared, it would be taken as an invitation to engage them in an inescapable conversation. They sat down, laughing, as the bus lurched into motion.

From the dock, they took a boat from where it had been tied up, but not locked down. Maria wondered if the owner had come looking for it yet, and what he might do if or when he saw that it was gone. Perhaps the police would come. She imagined two policemen in a rowboat of their own, struggling toward them from the shore, and laughed out loud.

It felt good to laugh. She hadn't done so in a long time. As she did, she could feel the tension in her body flowing out through her skin, draining away. Part of her wanted to look down and see if she could see it trickling into the water, though she knew that was ridiculous. After a moment, she calmed, exhaled slowly, and looked at Rebecca, who was still waiting for an answer to her earlier question.

"I don't know," she said. "I just felt like we needed to get away from everything, you know?"

Rebecca nodded and closed her eyes, looking up at the sun. It warmed her forehead and eyelids and cheeks and the bridge of her nose. Tiny trickles of sweat emerged and condensed at her temples like the water on the outside of a soda can.

Not that many days before, one of the boys at school saw something that someone had written about him, went into the bathroom, and swallowed a handful of pills. He was curled into a ball on the floor like a sleeping infant when his mother came home from work three hours later with takeout from the Korean barbecue place in town. She had served the food before going to his room to get him for dinner, and had been so shocked to find him like that that she stumbled out of the room and sat on the living room couch in silence until her husband got home. By that time, the entire house stunk of Korean food.

The girls saw the mother when the whole town gathered afterward. It was as though her pain had a repellant smell; it came off her in a contagious fog. If one didn't stay far enough away, then eventually one's world would turn gray and blue just like hers had. They ran away from the scene and ducked into a little bakery around the corner to eat fancy mini cupcakes until they'd almost forgot where they'd been. It was just a day off from school. Eventually they talked about it, and realized how confused they'd been by the whole thing. The idea that their lives might have a time limit, an ending, was shocking, and it took a while for the concept to sink in.

That was just one of multiple similar incidents among the students at their school that month. It seemed like there were fewer of them in class each day. Maria and Rebecca hadn't really thought much about the girl two grades behind them, who had fallen off her roof one night while her parents were out at dinner—she *was* a freshman, after all. It had been quite a story, though; her parents had driven home drunk and nearly ran over her body, flopped and bent as it was in the driveway.

Another kid set himself on fire in the center of the school's football field two hours before an important game was scheduled to start. Apparently, he'd been trying to send some kind of message. He'd painted a big banner with a slogan and laid it out on the grass, then knelt in front of it, soaked himself in gasoline, and lit himself on fire. Unfortunately, when he went up in flames, the pain was so great that he couldn't control himself and fell right on top of the banner. Between the gasoline and the paint, it was almost completely destroyed; only the very ends, which bore a large red S and two exclamation marks, remained intact, reducing his message to "S!!" Everyone was confused, the girls as much as anyone. His family chose to simply finish what he'd started, and cremated him.

The girls weren't totally convinced that the girl who fell off the roof was the victim of an accident. Who climbed up on a roof, after all? Maybe she had felt that her life was not going the way she wanted—a feeling Rebecca had voiced more than once herself to Maria that she was not living the life she wanted to live. But it didn't have to be the end of the road.

She remembered reading on some website a long

time ago, maybe as far back as middle school, that kids should keep in mind that someday their lives would be good, that adulthood held greater promise than a person's childhood. Neither of them was sure about that, but if one sat down and really thought about it, and weighed the good versus the bad, then life would seem all right. Parents weren't terrible people in general, and everyone had a good friend in someone.

It was simply confusing that those other kids weren't part of their lives anymore.

The things people seemed to worry about the most didn't bother Rebecca or Maria very much at all. Their parents and their neighbors and the other people they knew all cared so intensely about stuff: their cars, their houses, their clothes, even their pets. Maria knew a woman who adopted a new dog every year, depending on what the trendiest breed was. She would keep it, and seem to have a really loving relationship with it, but whenever people got excited over a new one, she would take her old dog to the pound and buy a new one from a breeder. It was like trading in a car. And somehow, when people like her suffered a financial setback, they treated it like an existential failure, as if having less money meant they were less worthwhile as people.

Why? They could still go outside. They could still have fun with their friends. They could still row a boat to the middle of a lake and just watch the birds fly by and the fish swim up to the surface of the water.

"We should keep going," Maria said. "We've been here long enough. It's getting hot."

It was. The sun was beating down on them and they were both sweating through their clothes. Rebecca didn't even bother reminding Maria that she'd promised to take a turn rowing; she just picked up the oars and began maneuvering the boat through the water.

They headed for the lighthouse. It was on a small island, far out in the center of the vast lake. It was impossible to see from one side of it to the other, much like an ocean. So maybe there was some justification for having a lighthouse there in the middle of it. Maybe boats coming across needed guidance. The girls didn't know, but they'd always heard about the island and the lighthouse, and now, in light of everything they'd learned and all they'd been through lately, they wanted to see it for themselves.

The island was a vaguely gray, slightly green bump in the distance. The lighthouse stuck up like a stubby pencil on one side. Maria pointed to it, as if Rebecca needed guidance, and the latter rowed harder.

It took nearly an hour to get there. By the time they did, Rebecca was so exhausted she thought she might not even have the energy to push them all the way to shore. But finally, they heard a scraping sound along the bottom of the boat as it struck the gravel of the shore. It stopped moving, and the tiny waves of the still lake lapped gently at its sides. Their arrival startled a few birds out of the trees; they flew away, cawing hoarsely. For a moment, Maria wondered if there were other animals on the island. It didn't seem very large, so it probably couldn't support bears or

wolves, but maybe large predators hid out there, waiting for dumb teenage girls to show up. Even if only
one human being came to the island each year, that
would be enough to feed a bear for a little while. She
hesitated before getting out of the boat.

Rebecca didn't, though. She laid the oars down
carefully, then leaned over, gauging the water's depth
by sight; it was shallow enough to see through. Tiny
fish, no bigger than tadpoles, zipped back and forth,
unaware of or unconcerned by her presence. Rebecca
took off her shoes, tucked her socks into them, and
gathered her shoes in her right hand before she lifted
her leg over the side of the boat. The water was surprisingly cool, considering how hot the sun was, and
only came up to her knees, barely touching the hem of
her dress. She stood perfectly still for a few minutes,
allowing the water to lower her body temperature. Her
sweat cooled, and she pinched her collar and flapped
it gently, unsticking it from her body.

Maria watched, waiting to see if something awful
would happen to her friend. Nothing did, and Rebecca
went ahead without even waiting to see what Maria
wanted to do. So Maria took off her own shoes and
socks and followed. She was wearing pants, and they
darkened as far as her knee as the water soaked into
the fabric. She hurried to dry land—wearing wet pants
was one of the worst feelings in the world. The two
friends stood side by side on the rocky shore.

They put their shoes on quickly because the rocks
were sharp and jabbing at the soles of their feet. The

lighthouse was only a few steps away, up a slight incline from the water's edge. It hadn't looked very large at first, even as the boat got closer to the island, but standing at its base and looking up to the top made it seem like a skyscraper. Maria led the way, and Rebecca followed right behind her.

It was made of gray stone that someone had painted white. The paint was flaking away in a lot of places, so whoever was in charge of upkeep was not doing their job. There was a single door made of old wood painted bright red, with a grimy brass knob that clearly hadn't been polished since the stones were painted. Maria examined it until Rebecca grew impatient, reached around her, and twisted the knob. The door opened with a crack and a loud squeal of rusted hinges. They both sucked in a breath out of surprise and fear, then gathered their courage and stepped inside.

"Hello?" Maria called. Her voice echoed up the spiral staircase to the top of the building. No one answered.

The interior was surprisingly well lit, a wide open space with a small kitchen at the far end: a refrigerator, a stove, a few cabinets, a sink, and a small table with two chairs included. There were only enough dishes for one person—a plate, a coffee cup, a fork, and a spoon—in a rack beside the sink. They were dry.

There was also a door directly opposite the one they'd come in. Rebecca opened it, too. It led to a bedroom with a single bed, a short chest of drawers, and a small bedside table with a couple of books stacked on top. The girls skimmed the titles; they were all mysteries, and they had all been read multiple times judging by the cracks in the spines and how the corners of many pages had been folded down.

Leaving the bedroom, they decided to climb the stairs. Maria went first this time. Their shoes clanged as they rose higher and higher into the lighthouse. Spaced evenly along all the walls were photos of people. Some were men, some were women, some were children. There were even some pictures of babies. Some of the adults were young, some were older; some had beards and some were clean-shaven. One man had hair that hung almost to his shoulders; another was totally bald, without even eyebrows, and wore round glasses that made his eyes look as big and round as a fish's. Under each portrait was a name and a span of time. The earliest portrait, at the very bottom of the staircase, was from nearly two hundred years ago. They thought maybe some of the people had been lighthouse keepers, but they couldn't be sure. Obviously, it took a certain type of person to endure that kind of extended solitude. Rebecca knew she couldn't do it. She'd go crazy in a week. But the people all looked happy and peaceful in their pictures, so maybe it wasn't so bad. At the top of the stairs, there was an empty frame with no name or dates underneath it.

The light at the top was gigantic, bigger than both of the girls together. There was a panel on the back for replacing the bulb when it burned out, and the front lens magnified the light, beaming it across the lake toward the town. There were heavy metal wheels that could turn the light from side to side, or up and down. Maria caressed the machinery with her fingers, but didn't adjust it in any way.

Next to the light, though, there was a telescope, and as soon as she saw it she ran over and spun it so it was facing the way from which they had rowed in order to get to the island.

"I can see our houses from here!" she shouted excitedly. It was true; the powerful instrument allowed Maria to see the street they lived on as though she were no more than a hundred feet away. Nothing much was going on. Someone's car backed out of the driveway and accelerated down the block, while another neighbor came outside with that year's dog on a leash.

She scanned the whole town. Everything looked calm and peaceful, though there was plenty of human activity. The silence made it all seem like a movie rather than real life. But as she looked at everyone going on with their days, driving here and there and walking in and out of stores, it all seemed strangely beautiful. She stared through the lens for what seemed like hours, examining different areas: her school, churches, neighborhoods she'd never even visited. Eventually, the sun began to set, and she took her eye away from the telescope's viewfinder. She wondered if she should turn on the light, then realized with a start that she hadn't heard Rebecca since she started looking out at the world. Where was she? Downstairs?

Maria called her friend's name, but there was no reply. She peered down the spiral staircase, then ran to the lighthouse window and looked outside. The boat was gone.

Panicking, Maria turned away from the window to look for her friend. She started down the stairs, but stopped when the pictures caught her eye again. She looked at the ones closest to the top of the stairs and suddenly recognized several of the kids from her school. Why would their pictures be here? She ran up and down the stairs, looking closely at all the photos. She recognized more of them—not many, but a few. They were her neighbors, her parents' friends, or just people she had seen around town, but at one point or another they'd disappeared. Vanished. Now it was all starting to click into place. Perhaps one day she, too, would disappear. And maybe someone would later see a picture of her and think, "Oh yes, I knew that girl."

THE LEADER

Whenever Victor went out into the world, he kept his eyes closed as much as possible. Movement was soothing, but the sights were too much. Victor's rituals allowed him to function; they were the reason he was still able to take any pleasure in life.

His destination drew close, but he had enough time to prepare accordingly. He opened his eyes, observing the other passengers on the trolley. They were all going to the same place, and they knew each other, or talked as though they did, expressing how excited they were and how much they looked forward to "becoming" and "moving forward." But none of them knew him, and hearing them talk to each other was like listening to a bunch of animals eager to be adopted and fattened up by a new owner. Not one mentioned what was actually going to happen: said owner having their balls chopped off.

The noise of their excited, happy conversations hurt Victor's ears. He couldn't believe he was going to have to live in the same house with these people.

He took his small notepad out of his front pocket, flipped past the ramblings on the first few pages to find what he was looking for: a list written in letters so bold that at first glance, one might think they were colored in ink.

TALK ABOUT YOUR FEELINGS
EXPRESS YOURSELF
IF YOU DON'T TELL THEM, THEY WON'T KNOW

The trolley stopped. Victor tucked his notebook away and let everyone else get off first. They all ran out like kids rushing to a drug store to get ice cream.

Victor took a final glance around the trolley once it was empty. It was cleaner than it should have been, and fancier. He thanked the driver in a low voice and hopped off. The hot, fresh air hit him, and he wished he had had the nerve to look outside before he exited the vehicle. There were no clouds, and he could feel the bright blue sky above—so far away, and yet it seemed close enough to touch. The sunlight washed away all of his mistakes, his bad dreams.

Victor followed the excited crowd. They were all walking slowly, peering at the beautiful scenery as if none of them had ever been outside before. He could hear them murmuring all sorts of exclamations and praise. *Yes, yes, it's gorgeous outside, now can you people keep moving?*

The farther they walked, the more colorful it got. Victor glanced around at all the beautiful flowers. He only knew the names of a few of them, like the daisies and sunflowers.

Even after several minutes, it didn't seem like they were anywhere near the big house. Victor looked down at his feet, his mind blank. The path eventually led to an open lawn, where it abruptly stopped. Somehow, he had wandered away from all the other people he'd arrived with; they were surprisingly far off in the distance, staring at the flowers and everything else, chattering among themselves like cartoon chipmunks.

There was a grand house at the far end of the lawn. Victor saw the sunlight shining off it and realized it was made entirely of gigantic panes of glass. Inside, steam coiled across the ground floor, almost ankle-deep. He could see people moving around, but what they were doing he couldn't understand. They walked back and forth, carrying mysterious objects here and there, and briefly conversing with each other before continuing on. The way they moved was strange; they wore blue robes that fell all the way to the floor, swirling the vapors with a soft hiss, and some of them seemed to drag their limbs behind them, as though their bones weren't fully solid. Some of them didn't look... He didn't know how to describe it. Right? Yes, that was it. They somehow didn't look *right*. It was their faces, he decided, and the way the skin sagged in loose baggy ripples, like it was too loose to contend with gravity. Their eyes seemed to move too quickly in their sockets, darting around like they were tracking flies in the air. None of them said anything to him, but Victor didn't like these weird people. He hoped they stayed away from him.

And yet, Victor walked closer to get a better look at a gigantic silver fountain just outside the house. Water shot high into the air from a wide-mouthed pipe in the center that looked like an abstract flower, then cascaded down into a ring of silver bowls. He smelled something sweet and flowery, a scent he'd encountered at home when one of his female family members took a long bath.

Near the fountain, all the other people had gathered into two groups. The men were on one side, and the women on the other. Victor counted quickly and realized that there were almost the same number of each, but there was one more woman. Then he realized that he was the last of the men's group and felt embarrassed for not noticing this before. His ears turned bright red as he joined his fellow men. He stood quietly in the back, hoping no one would ask him anything or even talk to him at all.

In front of them stood a man in a white robe who looked much older than those who moved about inside. In fact, he seemed older than anyone Victor had ever seen, but there was nothing stooped or short about him, the way a lot of old people become. He was tall and noble in appearance, and he gazed around at the house and all the people in it like they were his pets. He had long hair and a beard, both thick and silvery gray, and his eyes looked out at the world from within a bird's nest of wrinkles. Victor could tell he was the person in charge, the person they were all there to see.

"Good morning," the old man said in a calm voice. "Why have you come?"

All the people from the trolley—all, that was, apart from Victor—said as one, "We have come to move forward, to become our new and better selves."

No one had told Victor to memorize a special phrase; he felt embarrassed all over again. As always, he was the one who was wrong, the one on the outside. Depression buried him like a coating of wet clay. He resisted the urge to run away—he had no idea where he would go, anyway.

Now that he could see the old man up close, Victor could tell that there was something else different about him. It occurred to him that the old man wasn't human. And not in the same way that rich or famous people weren't really human. This was more elemental than that. This old man was genuinely a different species: a lizard, maybe, or a vulture that had pulled out all its feathers and learned to walk.

Victor looked at the ground again. He knew he was supposed to say something to make this old man like him, so he would be allowed to stay, but he didn't. He just waited for him to continue talking.

At length, the old man raised his hands, and everyone suddenly fell silent. "Come around," he commanded, and all the people in the group formed a circle around the base of the fountain.

They joined hands and started humming softly. The people on either side of Victor touched his hands, and because he knew he was supposed to join the circle, he did. He didn't start humming, though. The pattern was changing, so he could tell it was some kind of song, but he didn't know it.

"We have new arrivals here," the old man said in a booming voice that seemed to fill the entire world, without the help of microphones or amplification. It was louder than anything Victor had ever heard. It was like the man was speaking inside his brain—an unpleasant and uncomfortable feeling. He shook his head from side to side to make it go away, but it didn't. "These people wish to join us," the old man continued. Then Victor noticed that the people from inside the house had come outside and joined him. "They have traveled a long way to meet me and find out if they are acceptable to move forward and become something new. They wish to be judged. They think they are as we are. What do you think? Are they like us?"

Victor looked around. The people from inside with the weirdest faces wore suspicious expressions, like they definitely weren't looking for any new members at this time. Some of the others, who were both more humanoid in appearance and younger, seemed more welcoming. Victor wondered what that meant.

One of the older members of the house spoke up. "I do not think they are as we are," she said. Her eyes darted in all directions, as though she couldn't focus on any one thing. "They must be tested."

"Test," the crowd murmured in one voice. "Test. Test."

The old man smiled. "Tested they shall be. And if they are not as we are, they shall not remain." He clapped his hands together; the sound exploded in the air and Victor winced. The old man turned to the closest newcomer and said, "Are you prepared? Know that if you do not meet the challenge, there will be no second chance and no turning back."

The man nodded, and with lightning speed the old man grabbed him by the sides of his head, his hands covering the younger man's ears. With a surprising amount of force, he shoved the prospective member down to his knees before the fountain. The others all continued to hum and Victor just stared, wondering what was about to happen.

The old man released his grip, putting one hand on the back of the other man's neck before thrusting his head entirely under the water so quickly that there was barely a ripple or a splash. The man's arms flailed wildly, and then his hands gripped the rim of the fountain as his legs kicked at the ground. Without seeming to exert any effort at all, the old man held him under the water. Victor couldn't tell how long this went on, but he knew it was a while. Finally, the man's body stopped twitching and went perfectly still. The old man released his grip on the prospect's head, and the body slumped sideways to the ground.

"He was not one of us," the old man announced. "Remove him."

Two members of this strange society broke away from the circle and approached the body, grabbed under his armpits, and hauled him away. Victor didn't see where they went after that, but when they came back they rejoined the circle and no one said anything more about the man.

Each of the other new members was tested the same way the man had been. One by one, they stepped forward. When their heads were thrust under the water, most of them panicked, and most of them died. Only a few remained calm. They did not twitch or flail, and when the old man released them, they stood up as though nothing had happened at all. In fact, they all had calm smiles on their faces.

Victor watched without saying anything. Their deaths didn't upset him. He didn't know those people. He was afraid of being tested, though. Not because he thought he would fail and die, but because he didn't want to be put in front of other people. He'd rather be alone.

When everyone but Victor had been tested, the old man looked around the circle. "Is there anyone else who believes they are as we are?" Victor remained silent, trying to blend in, but the members of the group, and those who had survived the initiation, all stared at him.

Finally, one of the women pointed and said, "He has not been tested."

They all smiled in response, like they were at a dinner party and a surprise course had been laid on the table. Victor wanted to sink into the ground and disappear, but the old man signaled for him to come forward. He did, though he didn't want to, and was gripped by the neck, just like everyone before him had been. When his head was thrust under the water, Victor concentrated on not struggling. It was easier than he expected. He simply waited until the man released his neck, popped his head back out, and took a deep, cleansing breath.

"Welcome, all of you who are as we are," the old man said. Victor and the other new members stood silently in a line. There were only four of them; all the others had been taken away. Somehow, though, Victor didn't feel like he'd won anything. He felt ashamed that he was there at all, that there was something wrong with him that this old man was going to try and fix.

One of the group members stepped forward and handed the old man a copper pot with a paintbrush. The old man pulled the paintbrush out; it was covered in something red. When he stepped closer, Victor smelled it: blood. He gagged a little bit, but swallowed hard and managed not to throw up—even when the old man dragged the brush across his forehead, then down each of his cheeks. The blood mixed with the water still dripping from his hairline, and pink trickles ran down into Victor's eyes. He kept still and didn't wipe at his face, though he certainly wanted to. He kept still until he was invited inside the building, even though it was humiliating to walk around like that.

They were all taken inside and given beds. Victor was in a room with three other guys, two of whom were close to his own age and one who was older. The latter coughed a lot, and every time he did, Victor felt like he was standing too close. He wished he had a room to himself. Actually, he wished he had never come at all.

There was a square bundle of blue fabric lying on his bed. He picked it up and unfolded it to discover a strange garment, something between a robe and pajamas. Everyone else he was bunking with was already wearing theirs, so he put it on. The fabric was loose and soft, but he was so nervous and uncomfortable about everything else that it might as well have been made of sandpaper. He tugged at it and rubbed his arms and legs, where it scraped at his skin.

There was no food that night; the lights were turned out just after sundown, and everyone was expected to go to sleep immediately. The other people in Victor's room all fell into silent trances, their breathing as regular as that of horses in a barn. But he lay there, staring at the ceiling and wondering where he would go if he decided to run away. Eventually, after what seemed like hours, he fell asleep.

When he woke in the morning, he felt more tired and depressed than he had when he'd arrived. Everyone ate breakfast together in a giant refectory. Victor sat at the same table as the people he now shared a room with, and they were all given the same food: a bowl of some yellow-gray combination of oatmeal and pudding, a sliced apple, and a small glass of orange juice. He wasn't hungry, but he ate it all as fast as he could, taking big bites because he didn't want to get in trouble for not eating. He was soon finished, and had to just sit there and listen to everyone else talk about how happy they were to be there and how excited they were to "make progress." When he felt he couldn't take another moment, he left to explore the rest of the building.

He saw a quiet, deserted hallway and thought that was exactly where he wanted to be. Light came from under a door positioned a few feet down the hall, and as he crept closer, he heard strange noises—almost as though there were people inside being tortured. He turned the doorknob very slowly and peeked inside.

About ten people sat in a circle in the center of the room. They all wore their pajama robes, and they were all screaming and sobbing in terrible anguish. Their emotions were totally raw—every one of them looked more depressed than Victor had ever been in his life. All except for one: one person, obviously a more senior member of the group, wasn't crying or even upset. She simply watched the others wail and rock back and forth, some even leaning on each other for support, and she did nothing at all. She didn't seem disturbed in the least by the noise.

She smiled when she saw Victor in the doorway and said, "Come in, Victor."

He had no idea how she knew his name. He was sure he'd never seen her before, not even when he was baptized into the group. Just the sound of her speaking his name made his heart clench in his chest. He was more frightened of her than of the screaming, crying people. He didn't want to be in any group she was in charge of. He backed away and started to close the door.

"Come back, Victor!" she called. "Join us. You can't move forward unless you open yourself to change." He could barely hear her through the closed door and over the din, but figured that if he ever heard it again it would be too soon. He fled back down the hall as quickly as he could.

Once he saw another door and found the room it belonged to was empty, he ducked inside just to have a moment to himself. It was dark, and the air seemed cooler than anywhere else in the building. He put his back against the door and slid down until he was sitting on the floor. He lowered his head into his hands and closed his eyes, taking slow, deep breaths as his heart slowed down.

Just when he was starting to relax, he heard a scraping noise. He looked up; a teenage boy stood before him with a strange look on his face that suggested he didn't want to be in the house any more than Victor did. He wound his fingers together like an octopus's tentacles and shifted from one foot to the other, his eyes flickering all around like he saw things moving in the air.

"No," Victor said. "Stay away from me."

The boy's eyes focused on Victor then, and he realized that the kid hadn't noticed he was in the room before. But now he had. The boy stopped knotting his fingers and made a soft moan—out of fear or pain, Victor couldn't tell. He did wonder if the boy was going to start screaming like the others. Then he saw that his face didn't look quite right. It had lumpy, saggy spots, just like some of the other people he'd seen there so far. The boy raised his left hand to his cheek and started tugging at it: softly at first, then harder. He was dragging the skin and flesh down toward his neck...and it was stretching like bubble gum.

Victor was horrified. When the boy finally let go of the skin, it only sprung back halfway, where it then sagged and flopped. The boy continued to groan as his eyes rolled back in their sockets. Victor stood up slowly, trying not to attract the boy's attention, and reached back for the doorknob. He turned it quickly, sliding through as narrow a crack as he could manage to get back into the hall. As soon as the door shut, he turned around with the intention of heading back to the refectory.

The old man, the leader of the group, blocked his way. Victor jumped back and made a tiny shrieking noise.

"You are seeing things you should not see," the old man said. "These people are further along in their transition than you, and you are not prepared for that yet. You must honor the process, and move step by step. Come with me and I will take you where you need to be."

"I don't know if I belong here," Victor blurted out after a long pause. He couldn't even look the old man in the eye; he was staring resolutely at the floor.

"You don't belong out there," the old man said, reaching up and cupping Victor's face in his hands and gently tilted his head until they were looking into each other's eyes.

Try as he might, Victor could not hold the old man's gaze. Those eyes were too strange. They seemed to change color every second, swirling from gold to blue to black, and were speckled with a million tiny dots of light like stars in the night sky. But unlike the other group members, whose eyes constantly darted all around, the old man's gaze was as steady and unmoving as a lizard's. It felt to Victor as though the old man could look at him forever.

He glanced over the old man's shoulder and realized that many group members had joined them in the hallway. Victor was surrounded. He shuddered with a sudden wave of panic, but they were all smiling at him, looking at him like they had known him for years and liked him very much.

"Come, Victor," the old man said. "You are on a journey. You will become what you are meant to be, but it takes time."

"Become what you are meant to be," the group sang together. "Become one of us."

"No," Victor groaned. "No, I don't belong here. I don't want to be one of you."

"What do you want to be, then? Where do you want to go?"

"I don't know," he sobbed, backing away from the old man. He bumped into the wall, then pushed his way through the crowd of followers. There was a door that led out of the building just a few steps away. He ran to it, to his escape.

When he was outside, he looked around. Hadn't he just arrived yesterday? On a bright and sunny day? This world was totally different. The grass was dry and hard under his feet, and the flowers he had seen were now limp and dangling. He looked up at the sky. It was the color of mud, and the sun was a pale white marble within it. The air was as cold as a freezer's.

The old man and his followers hurried out behind him and surrounded him again. The old man placed one hand on Victor's shoulder.

"Come," he said. "Take your journey."

Victor's face felt strange. He reached up with one hand and gently rubbed at it, tugging the skin slightly. As if someone had flipped a switch, all of the fight left him, and he turned around and went inside.

THE BABY

The woman wouldn't stop screaming. Her howls echoed off the tiles of the hospital room. She screamed when she was alone. She screamed when a doctor or a nurse entered the room, or even came near her. Fear, pain, sorrow, frustration, and emotions so raw it wasn't possible to say what they were: she screamed until she was hoarse and out of breath, and no one did anything to stop her.

The doctors mostly stayed out of her room, opting to watch the monitors from the next room in order to learn everything they needed to know. She was safely tucked inside a steel cabinet painted white, like an oven, with her head protruding from a square hole at the top. Hundreds of wires, tied together in thick bundles like cable, extended out of the back and sides of the box and snaked over to the walls, where they disappeared into holes and connected to the various instruments and monitors in the next room. Each of those wires was connected to a sensor, which was attached to one part of her body or another, and she had to remain very, very still at all times to avoid corrupting the data. If she moved around, scratched an itch, or even sweated excessively, she could dislodge any one of the sensors. Then they'd have to open the box and reattach it without knocking any of the others loose.

It was enough to make anyone scream, and on top of everything she was very, very pregnant. For weeks she had felt like a bag someone was trying to kick their way out of.

Nearly a dozen doctors crowded the next room, which was really too small for all of them, and went through the data. It was hot and crowded, and their white lab coats were stained with sweat and other various substances. Each person had a separate task, but occasionally they had to consult with one another to verify data or establish a connection between two seemingly unrelated things.

The head of the obstetrics department was in charge, but he was not in a good mood. His patient's screaming made him tense and angry, and caused him to yell a lot at the other doctors, nurses, and medical technicians. That made them tense and angry in turn, and they often bumped into each other or bickered amongst themselves.

A nurse dropped a pen, which landed on the desk

of a technician, who glared at the nurse and swept it to the floor.

"Hey, what the hell?" the nurse snapped.

"Watch what you're doing," the tech replied, returning to his task without another glance.

The nurse grumbled under her breath and bent over to pick up the pen. Another nurse backed away from the screen she was looking at, bumped into the first nurse, and knocked her to her knees. They both yelped, and the second nurse almost fell over herself. This launched a series of small collisions throughout the crowded room, until almost everyone was either off balance or otherwise annoyed. It was like something out of a slapstick comedy.

Finally, the doctor in charge looked around at the chaos and began shoving and slapping everyone back into their positions. "Stop it, all of you!" he barked, grabbing a tech by the lapels. "Now, what do you have for me?"

"Her numbers are up since yesterday," said the tech, who was in charge of monitoring the woman's blood sugar.

"Why? Did we give her something different to eat?"

"No."

"What changed, then?"

"We don't know. Maybe something in her body is processing nutrition differently than it has been. Remember last week? Her salt retention spiked all of a sudden, for no reason, and then went back down again just as fast? We don't know what's going on in there. Nobody does."

The doctor rubbed his chin with one hand and his elbow with the other and stood perfectly still, closing his eyes so he could think. Everyone around him quietly went back to work, doing everything they could to stay out of each other's way and not cause any more trouble.

This patient's pregnancy had been a total mystery to him since the day she arrived at the hospital. Nobody knew who she was, or where she'd come from. He'd shown up for work one morning and she'd already been put in a room. She wasn't screaming then, but she was whimpering and wouldn't say a word to anyone. No one even knew what language she spoke at first. His head nurse told him that she had come in the front door, waddling like a penguin carrying a bowling ball in its fins and sweating like she'd run a marathon. They'd found her a bed, and it was immediately apparent that this was not an ordinary pregnancy. From the size of her belly, she should have already delivered, but the baby showed no sign of wanting to leave the womb.

The doctor came into her room that first morning and saw her lying on her back in the bed, her belly swollen like a beach ball, and decided to run a full battery of tests to learn as much as he could about her, her baby, and exactly what was going on. They put her into an MRI machine, but she barely fit. She grew louder and more panicked with every passing second, to the point that they couldn't complete the analysis. They injected her with glowing radioactive dye to see how her blood was flowing, and it was like her body drank it; it left no trace in her veins, and they learned nothing from that, either. Test after test failed or yielded inconclusive results, until finally they had no choice but to put her in the Box, which the doctor had been designing and experimenting with for several years but had never found the perfect subject for. This woman and her baby would be the one—two—to help him perfect his machine and get the answers he was after.

When they talked to her about going into the Box, they had explained that it would be comfortable, that the hospital staff would be monitoring her at all times, and that she would be in absolutely no danger. The look on her face said she did not believe them. When the nurse tried to take her arm to disconnect the IV and wires, she pulled away, not wanting to be touched. She inhaled deeply, obviously preparing to scream. They panicked, and ran out of the room to decide what to do. The doctor was insistent that they put her in his Box; he told the nurses that if they weren't able to get the job done, he'd have them fired and replaced with nurses who could. Finally, they all decided to wait until she fell asleep, at which point they would introduce a low-level anesthetic to her system and transfer her into the Box while she was unconscious.

That was three days ago, and from the moment she woke up with her head poking out of the box and thousands of wires leading away from her body and into the next room, she had not stopped screaming any longer than was necessary to breathe. The nurses were convinced that this was a very bad plan, but the doctor was certain that it was only a matter of time until the patient calmed down and the testing could really begin. For the moment, they were monitoring her numbers, making sure she got enough nutrients, and waiting.

And then, the screaming suddenly stopped. One moment no one could hear themselves think; the next, it was silent. The doctors, nurses, and technical staff didn't notice at first because they were all too busy being annoyed with each other and trying to convince the head doctor that theirs was the most important work going on. But eventually, one nurse perked up.

"Do you hear that?"

"I don't hear anything," the doctor said.

"Exactly." The nurse walked to the window, nudging a tech out of the way as she went, and looked into the next room at the Box. The woman appeared totally calm for the first time since she'd arrived. She was peering around, like she'd just woken up from a deep sleep and didn't know where she was, but she didn't seem upset at all. They looked at all the monitors and data to see if anything else had changed. The numbers were mostly the same; her blood pressure was okay, her heart rate was normal, there were no abnormal hormone levels in her blood... She seemed totally fine.

The doctor opened the door to her room very slowly, sliding his head in and looking at her for a long time without making a sound or any sudden movements. Finally, he gently cleared his throat and she swiveled her head as far around as she could to look at him.

"Hi," he said. "How are we doing today?"

"Only one of us is in a box, connected to a million wires," she said without smiling. "What do you mean, *we*?"

"Sorry," he said as he fully entered the room. The head nurse followed, making notes on a tablet. He walked around the Box to stand directly in front of her, but far enough away that she could look him in the eye without straining her neck. He kept his arms at his sides and his palms out, like he was trying to appease a lion instead of a pregnant woman. "How are *you* doing?"

"I don't know," she answered. "I'm worried."

"About what?"

"Myself. My baby."

"Does anything feel strange? Because according to our readouts, you seem perfectly normal."

"I don't know what strange would feel like," she said. "I've never been pregnant before."

"Well, what is the baby doing?"

"Talking to me," she said. "It talks to me in my dreams."

The nurse tightened her grip on her tablet so she wouldn't drop it. Those things were expensive.

"What do you mean?" the doctor asked, all the while trying to maintain a straight face. "You dream that your baby wants to tell you something?"

"No, it just tells me things," she said.

"What kind of things?"

"Like how it wants to climb trees. It wants to swim in the ocean. It wants to pet our dog."

"You keep saying 'it.' Is it a boy or a girl?"

"It won't tell me."

"Can you...talk back to it?"

"I'm not sure. I think at it, like trying to send it a message with my mind, but it never really answers me or reacts to what I mean to say. It's like it just wants to express its own opinions and doesn't care what I think." She paused. "And, honestly, I'm not sure I like its personality. It's pretty egotistical. When it first started talking to me, I told it all the time that I loved it, but it never says it loves me back."

"Do you know when you're due? How long have you been pregnant?"

"I'm not sure," she said. "The whole thing has been like a dream. I feel so disconnected from myself, like the only part of me that still exists is the part that's feeding the baby while it grows. I barely talk to my husband about anything other than the baby anymore. I used to read books and watch movies and leave the house to go have fun and experience life. Now I don't do any of that. I just sit around on the couch and get bigger and bigger, and listen to the baby tell me about all the things it's going to do once it comes out. It's not what I imagined it would be like at all."

The doctor and the nurse left the room to join the rest of the team on the other side of the wall.

"So what do you think?" the doctor asked.

"The baby's talking to her in her dreams? She's obviously crazy," one technician said. "We should induce labor and get that baby out of her so we can give it to someone who'll be able to take proper care of it."

"No," a nurse said, shaking her head violently, like she'd just heard the worst idea ever. "No, we need to find a way to monitor the communications between her and the baby. There must be some way."

"So you think she's telling the truth?" the doctor asked. "You think the baby is really communicating with her?"

"I'm not sure," the nurse said. "But we should at least test the theory."

The technician who had suggested removing the baby became angry. He said that babies were precious things—not many people in Brookville had them anymore, and the ones that were born often died very soon afterward—and to give one to a crazy person, who didn't even seem to like it very much, was a mistake. She might harm it, and then where would they be? He stood up from his desk and started pacing, bumping into people and waving his arms as his face grew red and sweaty. Eventually, he came to a stop right in front of the nurse and began screaming in her face. She shouted back that he was an idiot, that the bond between mother and child, even if it was unwilling on the mother's part, was the most important thing in the world, and that no one should break it unless they absolutely had to. And besides, what if she wasn't crazy? What if the baby really was talking to her? They didn't know.

The doctor tried to step between them. "Calm down," he said to the technician.

"I'm perfectly calm!" the man yelled with so much force that he spit all over the doctor's face and lab coat. "You of all people know how many babies we've lost just this month! We need to get that thing out of her! It belongs to us now!" He turned and ran out of the room, the doctor on his heels as he burst into the patient's room and stomped over to the Box. "Give us your baby!"

"What do you mean?" the woman asked, startled.

"Give it to us!" he shouted. "Push it out right now, or we're going to take it from you!"

"No! You can't have my baby!" She saw the doctor and the two big, muscular male nurses that followed them in. They grabbed the technician by his arms and lifted him up off the ground. His feet were twitching like he'd just run off a cliff, but hadn't stopped or started falling yet. They dragged him away, and then only the doctor and the woman were left in her room.

"I'm very sorry about that," the doctor said sheepishly.

She looked at him with wide eyes. "I think the baby wants to come out now."

"Really?" The doctor was immediately excited, the drama from before completely forgotten. He looked in the direction of the other room, then ran out without another word to his patient.

The nurses and technicians were all very agitated in the next room.

"There's something going on," one of them said. "The numbers all started going up at the same time.

Her pulse, her blood pressure—everything."

"She says the baby wants out. We better get her out of the Box," the doctor said, and pressed a button to summon the orderlies, who would take the woman upstairs to give birth.

They wheeled a bed into the room and unlocked the Box. The woman rose very slowly, peeling wires off of her arms and legs and belly and neck one at a time, dropping them into the bottom of the Box. It took several minutes, but finally she wore nothing but a hospital robe. With the help of the hospital staff, she stepped out of the Box and moved to the gurney, her gigantic belly rising up like a pulsing beach ball.

The doctor leaned over and said, "We're going to take you upstairs now, and we'll get the baby out as quickly as possible. Is there anything we need to know? Is it talking right now?"

"No," she said. "It's not saying anything at all."

It took seventeen hours. All the technicians and nurses gathered in the observation room, looking down on the woman and the medical team as they encouraged her to push and breathe and do all the necessary things to get the baby out of her body. She gritted her teeth and sweated and groaned and pushed as hard as she could, and little by little, the baby was born.

It was a girl. She came out with her eyes open, looking all around like she was checking to make sure everything was where she expected it to be. She looked the doctor right in the eye, and he saw something in those blue eyes that he had never seen for as long as he'd been delivering babies.

He took a deep breath, and without a word to the nurses or the girl's mother, he picked the baby up and held it at eye level, so they were face to face.

"Hello," he said. "How are you?"

"Hello," the baby replied in a voice like a kitten's meow.

SHOWTIME

S he sat backstage in her dressing room, staring into the mirror though she hardly recognized her own reflection

Everything about her had changed since she was first cast in the play. She barely remembered the girl who had auditioned. She'd shown up at the theater nervous, wearing the best clothes she owned at the time, clothes she would now be ashamed to even donate to a thrift store. She would have taken any role at all. She'd had a passion for theater since she was a little girl, and by the time she auditioned, it was the only thing she wanted out of life.

She had been struck by the dazzling beauty of the theater, all decked out in maroon and gold and shining like a temple. It felt like she should have entered on her knees. She was greeted by an assistant with a headset and a clipboard, then taken backstage to wait with maybe a hundred other girls.

One at a time, they stepped out onto the stage, said a line or two, paused to listen to comments from the writer, the producer, and the director, then either delivered another few lines or went backstage again. She was terrified, because when the other girls returned, they all looked shocked, like something terrible had happened to them out there. A few of them were crying; others looked numb, like something inside them had broken. None of them spoke to anyone. They just gathered their things and left the theater alone.

Finally, it was her turn. She walked through the door leading from the backstage hallway, with its gold walls and maroon carpet, to climb the few steps to the stage. The lights were blinding; she couldn't see anyone in the audience at all. There was an X taped in the center of the stage, and she knew that was where she was supposed to stand, so she walked up to it and planted her feet firmly, trying to find the confidence she knew she didn't possess.

"Hmm," said someone in the darkness, almost like they were considering a menu, deciding what to have for dinner.

She paused to let her eyes adjust. After a few seconds, she could see the people who ran the show sat a few rows back. They were dressed in beautiful clothes, all gold and white with pearls to accent and catch the light. They looked so happy to her, so pleasant and inviting.

"Go ahead," the man who ran the theater said.

She began speaking the lines she had memorized, but she barely had a chance to finish a sentence when the one that had sounded like a discerning diner said, "Yes." It was soft, like she wasn't meant to hear, but she did. Still, they hadn't interrupted her outright, so she kept going. She moved off the mark, becoming more involved in her performance and delivering the lines with real passion. She paced back and forth across the stage, barely noticing that she'd gotten deeper into her monologue than any of the other actresses before her had.

Finally, the man in charge of the space said, "Wait—stop."

She stopped in the middle of her sentence and returned to the X. She stood perfectly still, waiting to hear what they had to say. It was only at that point that she realized how long she'd been talking. The monologue she'd memorized was meant to last nearly five minutes, and she'd gotten almost to the end before they'd cut her off. Her breath grew short, and she started sweating. Suddenly, she was even more nervous than she'd been when she was waiting to go on.

"Yes," the first man said again.

She held her breath, waiting to hear a real confirmation before she thanked anyone for the role.

"Yes," he said a third time with a tone of finality.

"Congratulations," the other man said.

It had taken her a moment to realize what that single word meant. She was the one. The part was hers!

And it had been hers every night since. She had an

understudy, in case she was ever sick, but she'd never met her, and she'd never missed a performance.

Since she'd joined the cast of the play, she had changed in so many ways she couldn't even describe. It was like the whole world was changing. The way the show was written, and rewritten, changing subtly over time—a few lines here, a scene there—caused her to alter her performance, so she wasn't really playing the same character she'd originally been hired to play. That woman had evolved. She was more passionate, and for the last few months she'd been angrier, too, confronting injustice in a way that the actress had to admit she found a little bit cathartic. All that yelling and raging allowed her to get her personal feelings out of her system.

But had she had those feelings before the script called upon her to be angry? Where was the line between the role and her actual self? And was the outside world really different, or did she perceive it differently because of what went on inside the theater every night?

When she'd been cast, they'd asked her if she wanted to change her name. Except it hadn't really been a question; the producer had told her that he didn't think she had a star's name. He said it in such a way that he made her angry; it was like he thought he was doing her a favor, like he thought she *could* be a star, if only this one thing about her was different. She asked him what he had in mind, and he suggested one. She hated it, and told him so. He made another suggestion, which was even worse than the first. She actually laughed at that one; his ears turned bright red and his eyes narrowed. For a moment she was convinced she'd lost the job she'd only just been given, but then the writer came over, and, with a smile, asked her what she was laughing about.

"He wants me to change my name," she said, giving him her best first date smile.

"Oh," the writer said. "Well, it's not a terrible idea. What names has he suggested?"

The producer repeated the first two names, and the writer made a sour face at both of them. After the second name, he nudged her with his elbow—his way of saying that he was on her side.

"How about this?" He offered a name of his own, which she immediately liked much better. She looked up at him and nodded, smiling. He turned to the producer and said, "There you go. That's her new name. It'll look great on the posters."

The producer nodded and walked away.

But the new name had been just the beginning. After she'd been performing for almost a year, the writer and producer asked her for a meeting. Sitting in her dressing room, the two of them stood over her so that she was tucked into the corner like a child being punished. They told her that they had received audience feedback suggesting she was looking older, and that they thought it would be a good idea if she had some minor facial work done. Nothing extravagant, just a few adjustments here and there. She wouldn't even need to miss a performance; it could be done as an outpatient procedure, and any post-op marks would get covered with makeup that night. She hadn't known what to say, but refusing hadn't seemed like an option. So she'd agreed, and they made an appointment for her with a plastic surgeon, who tightened up the skin around her eyes, smoothed out some lines by her mouth, and—since she was there anyway—gave her the tiniest, subtlest nose job.

That was about fifteen operations ago. Each time, it was just a small change, just a tweak of an eyebrow or a little bit of filling in of the lips, but after so many years and so many procedures, she didn't recognize the woman looking back at her in the mirror. When she tried to shut her eyes and imagine what she looked like when she first got this job, she realized that even her memory was no longer accurate. She couldn't remember her original face; she could picture one from five, six, maybe even ten operations ago, but the one she'd been born with was gone forever.

The play itself had changed greatly since she was cast. The writer locked himself in his office every day from morning until night, only emerging to get coffee or occasionally food. When he did come out, he locked the door behind him so no one could sneak in to see what he was writing. But every week, sometimes more than once, he would present her with new pages that she would have to learn before that night's show. Sometimes the changes were minor, but other times he'd reworked entire scenes, changing the relationships between characters and making them angrier or more sexually charged than they'd been in the past. And, just as with her surgeries, these changes added up over time, snowballing until it was no longer the same story at all.

She never liked the changes. There had been versions of the play that she felt were improvements compared to the original, but they always ended up going in a wrong direction, and some were actually offensive to her. She knew that, as an actress, it was her job to translate the words into action and make the writer's ideas real. She understood that her creativity would always be in service of his, but there were times when she felt like the writer was out to get her.

There were multiple occasions when she'd expressed discomfort with something she had been asked to say or do in a rewrite. In one such case, she had been handed the pages only a few minutes before going onstage and wasn't at all sure she had them memorized by the time the curtain went up. Not long after she'd complained about the sudden change, she'd gotten a new set of scenes that depicted her character in an extremely negative light. She was portrayed as bitchy, as someone who had nothing positive to say to or about anyone else in the play. But when she took her concerns to the writer, asking him if he had some problem with her and what she could do to smooth things over, he just shrugged and said that there was nothing wrong, that he was just responding to audience feedback and writing what people wanted to see and hear. Since the actress didn't know that the producers were soliciting feedback from the audience, she was never sure whether or not to believe him, but she didn't really have a choice. She needed the job.

She didn't really think they were responding well to the audience's demands, though. She couldn't be sure, but it didn't seem to her that the play was as popular as it was when it debuted. The audience still applauded at the end, but she could remember receiving standing ovations for early performances. Now, there were nights when it seemed like many of the people in the seats felt it was their duty to clap, not that they actually wanted to.

The people who were most interested in seeing the play were all incredibly rich, wearing fancy clothes and covering their faces with eerie white masks ringed with jewels. One of the people who worked at the theater had told her that the masks were images of former lovers the rich maniacs had murdered, but she'd walked away laughing, unsure whether to believe it or not. Sometimes, even with the house lights out while she delivered her lines, she'd occasionally catch a glimpse of them, and it took everything she had not to panic and lose her place. She could hear them, too—talking about horrible things they wanted to do to her. Some didn't even whisper.

There were several different types of weirdos. She'd had a few stalkers, men who had shown up outside the theater at the end of the night wanting to talk to her, meet her, date her. One man had come every night for two weeks, always with a single rose. The first night he'd come, she'd politely taken the flower. When he returned the next night, she had ducked back inside the theater before he could see her. She had told the theater manager that there was a creep stalking her, and he showed her a secret door that the public didn't know about. It led to a short, dark tunnel that took her out to the street a block away from the theater. She used that to come and go now, every morning and every night, and she disguised her appearance. She had one wig she wore when she arrived, and a different one for when she left. One day she came to the theater after a few days off and there was a man living in her dressing room, curled up under the table where she put on her makeup. She'd screamed and told the manager, but he just laughed. He said she should be flattered, that it showed just how devoted the public was to the play and to her. He offered her a new dressing room, but it didn't even have a lock on the door.

Some fans frightened her even if they didn't try to talk to her. They sat in the audience, staring blankly at her throughout the entire performance without even blinking. There were certain points in the play, especially when the action was quiet or subtle, that she could even tell that these obsessive fans were synchronizing their breathing with hers. When she inhaled, there was a soft, but audible hiss from the audience; when she exhaled, there was a collective whoosh. The first time this happened, it disturbed her so much that she almost forgot to breathe. It took a conscious effort not to pass out.

Other fans had gotten surgery to look like her. They couldn't afford the type of doctors she could, though, and they couldn't keep up with her changing features. So they looked like roughly sculpted versions of what she'd looked like a year or two earlier. And some of them were a lot older than she was, or heavier, so the operations didn't have the same results. The worst ones looked like melting wax versions of her. Frankly, she thought it was horrible. She had asked the stage manager if he could stop turning on the lights at the end of the show, when the cast came out to bow and say good night; she didn't want to see those mutant reflections of herself staring back at her, clapping, sometimes crying. But the producer told her that those people had paid good money to see her and she was going to have to give them what they'd come for.

That wasn't the worst of it, though. Lately, she had begun to see people sitting in the audience with mannequins that looked like her. They were exactly her height and sculpted to look like her; some of them were in her character's clothes, while others were in fancy outfits that she'd never worn in her life. It was obvious that these people had dressed the mannequins up in clothes that held some significance to their own lives: maybe a prom date, or someone they worked with but never had the courage to talk to. Those fans terrified her most of all. The first time she'd seen one of the mannequins, she'd burst into tears and run offstage.

She'd nearly collided with the writer, who grabbed her by the shoulders and asked what was wrong with a look of real concern on his face. When she told him, he'd stuck his head out by the side of the curtain and scanned the audience until he saw the thing. He'd turned back to her with a wicked smile.

"Wow, that's amazing. You think if we sold those at the merch table, a lot of people would buy them?" He'd laughed until he noticed that she was crying even harder, actually shivering with fear. Then he'd wrapped one arm around her shoulders and said, "Don't worry, we'll never do that." She'd sniffled a little and smiled up at him, but she wasn't at all sure she believed him.

A knock at the door jolted her out of her thoughts. "Come in," she said.

The producer and the writer entered the room. The writer was carrying a few sheets of paper, which he handed to her with a smile. "I've added a new scene. I think you'll really like it."

She took the pages, smiling back at him. She was a good actress; she was sure she could convince him that she liked whatever it turned out to be. She glanced at it quickly. On the first page, the male lead was yelling at her. She put the pages down on the table and turned to the producer, offering him a brief greeting.

"Hi," he said. "Full house tonight. They really love you out there."

She smiled and said nothing.

"I've been thinking," he went on. "A lot of young models these days have really sharp, arched eyebrows.

I think that would look wonderful on you, give you a modern, up-to-date look that the audience would respond well to. We're gonna make an appointment for you—maybe next week? It'll look great, I'm sure of it."

She smiled and said nothing.

"Well, have a good show," the writer and producer said, almost at the same time, then looked at each other and laughed. They walked out and shut the door behind them.

She looked into the mirror again. Who was that person? She didn't know, but she didn't like her. Not anymore.

She reached into a drawer and pulled out a towel she'd brought from home the day before. Wrapping it around her hand to protect her knuckles, she punched the big mirror with one short, fast blow. The glass cracked from top to bottom, and several razor-sharp shards, as long as carving knives, fell to the tabletop. She picked one up and slowly raised it to her cheek.

THE STORIES

The world was getting smaller and smaller. Nature made noises that no one else could hear. Her mind was ringing; she felt like she'd lived for centuries. Exhaustion was like a physical pain, striking hard all over her body. She could feel someone behind her, staring at her, and it wasn't just some kind of psychic intuition, but an almost physical feeling on her skin. It wasn't a blank stare, either. Whatever was staring at her had feelings, feelings exactly like her. She knew its glowing, owl-like eyes all too well, and realized it was looking for its next home. Its next life. Its next existence.

Each of her days and nights were like this. The black and white world surrounded her in all directions, sucking the creativity right out of her, its needle buried deep in her skin. She was used to an influx of luxurious ideas every day, to the point that she'd felt spoiled. But they came less frequently now, and left less of her behind when they were gone.

The feeling of those glowing eyes—Marcel's eyes— grew more intense on her back, like the room was slicing open.

"Where are you gonna put me in?" Marcel demanded. He ran out of the darkness and leapt in front of her. She flinched. "When am I gonna get a story?" he screamed. Marcel got angry quickly. "I've been locked away too long!" His spit struck her watery eyes. Marcel then grabbed her face in his thick, rough hands. She felt his veins popping up beneath his skin. "Say something, you spoiled monster!"

Marcel let go of her and slapped her across the face like he wanted to pound every last drop of his own pain into her. A tear rolled down her face, but Marcel's harsh glare into a smile and started to laugh. The others watching from the darkness joined him.

Mary woke suddenly, as though someone had thrown a bucket of water over her. She sat up in bed and shook with residual fear, reassuring herself that she'd been dreaming again. In the shadows, she swore she could still see some of the threatening figures, as though they'd wandered into the real world just to torment her. She reached out to try and recapture them, but then they were gone. Words had come to her, glowing and floating in midair like neon signs in a cartoon, and she knew that even though she couldn't remember any of them or arrange them into sentences, she would be convinced for the rest of the day that if she had only been able to write them down they would have been the most brilliant, beautiful sentences she'd ever written.

The whole house was dark, and painted in shades of black and white. She had never seen the world in color, had never spoken about that to a living person.

Was that a condition of her vision, her unique way of seeing the world, or was the entire universe black and white? That would be so binary: on/off, yes/no, do/don't, love/hate. That wasn't how she wanted the universe to be, and it didn't match the photographs that NASA published of deep space, as seen by tele-scopes. But that meant nothing, because someone had told her that NASA added those colors into the pictures to help people identify and distinguish what was there. Her stories felt a bit like that; they were a way of looking at things, but she knew there were other ways and that she'd essentially added color to help people understand hers.

She looked around, waiting for her eyes to adjust to the gloom. Soon she would be able to see the few objects in her room—the desk, the chair, the door—and get up and move around without bumping into anything.

But then there was a bright flash of light. It only lasted a second or two, but it illuminated the room like a nuclear explosion. Mary yelped and shut her eyes as fast as she could, but it was too late. Dancing spots appeared on the inside of her eyelids, and she knew she would have to wait long minutes before she adjusted to the dark again... And then there would probably be another flash. She was used to this—it happened again and again every day, but always at unpredictable intervals.

"Good, you're here," said a voice, making her jump. A young boy stood in the corner of her room. His clothes were stained with what could have been blood, but a second glance told her it was grease and motor oil. In an instant, she recognized him. He was forever building machines in the basement of his house.

"What do you want?" she asked.

"I don't like my story," he said. "Fix it."

She slumped back down in bed. "What should I change it to?" Mary asked in a voice much like an exhausted mother at the end of a long day. And like a mother, she was indulging him. She wasn't going to change anything. His story was his story and, if he didn't like it, well, tough. Lots of people didn't like their stories. "Tell me what you want to happen."

"I don't know," he whined. "You're the writer. But I don't like it how it is now, so fix it."

"Go away," she said, flapping her hand at him like she was shooing away a cat.

"No. Fix my story!" He punctuated his demand with a stomp of his foot.

She'd been working on his story for weeks. When she first came up with the idea of a boy building a robot version of his brother, it had seemed so strange and thrilling. But from the minute she'd started writing about the two brothers, one or the other was always complaining.

"I don't want to be killed."

"Why am I turning him into a robot?"

"This story is stupid."

Mary was sick of it. It was a good idea, but they wouldn't leave her alone. All she wanted now was to finish the story so they'd disappear out of her head.

She crossed the room with long, quick strides, keeping her eyes half-shut in case there was another bright flash. She didn't want to be blinded and lose more time that she could spend working. Pulling out her chair and sitting down in one smooth motion, she flipped open her notebook and started writing, barely allowing herself time to think about the words before she scrawled them onto the page. Her handwriting was wild, a swooping mess; it didn't matter. No one else would ever read this version. As long as she knew what it said, that was enough.

The door to her room swung open with a wrenching creak. She glanced up and saw a creature unlike anything she'd ever seen before, which was no surprise because no one anywhere had ever seen anything like this creature before. It had a twisted face, and its skin was like the bark of a white oak tree. With every move it made, layers of its rough skin peeled away, and it grabbed at its own flesh to speed the process along. Growths all over its body looked like snail shells. From a distance, they would look like wounds inflicted by something stabbing it over and over. It had an underbite and its teeth were a deep, nutlike brown color, as though made out of split wood. It had seven eyes, all clumped so close together that she wondered whether it could even focus properly, or if it only saw some kind of mosaic-like image everywhere it looked. It made a noise somewhere between a gurgle and a roar, like a dog trying to choke down a piece of meat that was too big for it to swallow.

She shuddered in spite of herself, but kept writing. Even though it was her imagination that had given it life, she hadn't expected it to be quite so vivid and repulsive. It continued to thump and drag its heavy, contorted limbs around the room, bumping into furniture and looking for something to attack and eat even as it tore at itself, leaving a trail of shredded hide behind. It swiped at her and missed by quite a bit, but when it whooshed past her, she felt some of her energy go with it. Her head slumped toward the desk, and she had to struggle to raise it again. Each story took something out of her and she wondered if, eventually, when the last story was written and the last notebook closed, she would completely run out of energy and simply die on the spot.

For some reason, the little boy didn't seem afraid of the monster. He just watched it stumble around the room. Eventually, though, its movements slowed, first gradually and then suddenly it stopped, frozen in the middle of the floor. She had lifted her pen from the page, unable to come up with the next event. She closed the notebook just as another bright light flashed. She shut her eyes tight, but it was too late; they were seared, and the inside of her eyelids pulsed with pain. When she reopened them, the creature was gone.

Beyond her room, she could hear the sounds of people moving around and going about their morning routines. Her mother and father always conversed in soft, friendly tones as they prepared breakfast together. When it was ready, her mother would come and knock on her door, inviting her to eat with them. Well, more often than not, she'd pound on the door with her fist and shout, "Get up, it's time for breakfast!"

As though feeding her daughter was some kind of punishment, a duty imposed on her.

Mary didn't want to come out, anyway. They would only ask her if she'd accomplished anything lately or, worse, what she was planning to do with her future. As though it was up to her. As though there was some grand world of opportunities out there, just waiting for her. They didn't understand just how much her work took out of her—that every time she finished a story and dropped it into the world's hungry mouth, a piece of her went with it. And yet, at the same time, when she looked back at what she had written, every drop of pain that had gone into its creation was just as present as always. She could never let go, never move forward. It was like having her blood drained, mixed with poison, and pumped right back into her body.

She opened the notebook again, to a different section this time, and stared at the densely scrawled paragraphs there. "Ugh."

"I know," said the man standing behind her.

She looked over her shoulder at him. He was running his thick fingers through his messy dark hair. In his other hand, he held a pair of pliers, and in the jaws of the pliers was a single tooth, its roots still bloody like he had just yanked it out of his own mouth. His spoke in a sort of choking grumble; he couldn't form words properly. Even if he'd had all his teeth he would still have been kind of dense, and more than a little bit crazy. He paced in tight circles, his shoes squeaking against the floor—strange, considering Mary's room was carpeted. But wherever he was from, the floor must have been made of hard wood, so his heavy, battered and stained boots practically sanded the floor as he walked.

"You want out, don't you?" she asked him, as though he was a dog who needed to be taken outside to relieve itself.

He grunted and nodded, pacing faster. But then he shook his head. "No. Too much to do. Have to stay."

She looked down at the page and read what was written there. Then she scrubbed out a few lines with forceful strokes of her pen, digging into the paper like the words were buried beneath its surface, waiting to be excavated. She turned three whole lines into a thick black smear, then wrote a few words—short phrases, not full sentences, as those would come later—underneath.

"Sorry," she said. "You've got to go outside. It doesn't make sense unless you leave."

The man shuddered and groaned. He was afraid. He tried to explain to her that he needed to stay, that he was important, that what he was doing in his room had meaning and purpose. He begged her to leave him alone, to leave him where he was.

"I get it," she said. "I do. But I promise, it's really important that you get out of there. I'm gonna have someone come and get you. And I'll give you a friend you can visit."

She wrote down a few more notes and flipped the page over. He disappeared, muttering like he wasn't sure about that idea, but he'd trust her.

Mary crossed her ankles beneath her chair and felt a soft bump. Whatever she had kicked moved away; she heard a tiny rustling sound and peeked down. It was a turtle. Its dark green shell was wet, as if it had just come out of a pond or a tank. As it retreated under the desk, avoiding her foot, she saw more turtles hiding out there. She slipped out of the chair and squatted down on the floor, watching the turtles crawl around and climb over each other in search of—food? A slightly different patch of floor? Another turtle they liked better? She smiled.

Even when the light flashed, she didn't care. Down low, under the desk, her eyes weren't hurt as badly as they ordinarily would have been. She only had to blink a few times to get her vision under control again. But as she watched the turtles, she realized that, though she found them relaxing and pleasant, she didn't really have anything to say about them. Occasionally one of

them would look at her, but they showed no real interest in her beyond that. To them, she was an object, no
different than a rock or the chair. They crawled over
and around each other, silent and expressionless.
They opened their beaks from time to time, but no
sound ever came out.

Suddenly, a phrase occurred to her. Five—no, seven
words, perfectly sequenced. She jumped up and began
pacing around the room. Behind her, unattended, the
turtles vanished, one by one and then all at once. As
she paced, faster and faster, careful to avoid bumping
into the bed or the chair, she considered the phrase.
What did it mean? It was as though she held a diamond up to the light, turning it around and around
and tilting it this way and that to watch it glitter and
gleam. She tried rearranging the words in her mind,
but they were exactly right just as they were. Trying
to improve the sentence was like trying to pull the
links of a steel chain apart with her fingers; it wouldn't
break, wouldn't budge.

She realized after a few minutes that the phrase
had come from her dream. It was one of the strings
of words that had hovered before her eyes when she
first woke up, but then fluttered away. Now they had
returned to her. She flopped back onto the bed, her
head landing on the pillow with a soft puff of air.
Perhaps, she thought, if she returned to where she
had been when the words had first appeared, they
would grow stronger in her mind and expand all on
their own. Soon, she might have an entire paragraph,

then multiple paragraphs, then a whole page. Before long, she would have an entire story. All she had to do was wait patiently, and the words would come.

Mary closed her eyes, stretched her legs out, folded her ankles right over left, and crossed her arms over her chest like a vampire in a coffin. Immediately, she felt a wave of relaxation come over her. The seven words stayed perfectly still on the screen of her mind. She was certain that an eighth would arrive soon, then a ninth, and then more and more.

But they didn't, so she began to consider the phrase as it was. It was descriptive, but not declarative. It had no verb, so no action was implied. It was the beginning of something, or at least she thought it was. Perhaps it was the beginning of the end. What if it was the start of the first sentence of the last paragraph of the story? How would she arrive at that point? She began to think about the phrase as a goal to be reached, a finish line rather than a starting point. Was there a world in which this phrase was exactly the right description for a moment, or a mood?

All around her, the world shimmered as she considered these seven words, what she would write before and after them. Loosely formed figures materialized in the corners of the room, took a step forward, then vanished in a cloud of vapor that would then rearrange itself into a new form for her to consider: a whale, a tree, a house. The white light flashed, but Mary's eyes were shut and it didn't matter. The flash seemed less bright, somehow, when it couldn't hurt anyone.

The monster and the man with the pliers reappeared and stood over the bed, looking down at Mary where she slept. They looked at each other, and seemed mutually disturbed by what they saw; they backed away, casting worried glances back and forth. Their postures were tense, as though an attack was imminent, though neither one seemed aggressively inclined toward his neighbor.

Mary opened her eyes again and sat up. The sentence was no closer to being finished than it had been when she'd laid down. But now she had an idea. She thought that if she wrote it down on paper, she could concentrate on it and then the story would begin to fill in around it.

She looked up at the monster and the man with the pliers, and a third person who had joined them: a very old man wearing a hospital gown. He looked frightened. She didn't know why he was there. She'd resolved his issues for him quite a while ago. "What do you want?"

"I made the wrong choice," he said.

"No, you didn't," she said. "I chose for you, and I don't doubt my decision. Now go away, all of you. I'm busy."

She stood up and passed through all three of them like mist. A turtle crawled past her foot; she looked down at it and shook her head. It, too, disappeared.

Sitting at her desk and flipping the notebook open to a blank page, she wrote down the seven words, exactly as they had appeared in her mind. As she did it, the entire house seemed to shiver and ripple, as though someone had poked the surface of a pond with their finger.

She stood up. This was a crucial step; this was progress. She knew the rest would come, but for the time being she could give herself a short break. She'd go downstairs and talk to her parents, see if there was anything good to eat.

Mary opened her bedroom door; it creaked as loud as a scream. The stairwell was pitch black, but she knew exactly how many steps led to the kitchen. Still, she descended cautiously, with one hand on the banister at all times and her ears listening carefully. There was nothing. The house was silent as she walked into the kitchen. No one and nothing was there. The cabinets were empty. There was a refrigerator at one point, but it had been dragged out the door; the marks on the tile floor were clearly visible, dark scuffs leaving a trail through the dust no one had swept for a long time. The kitchen table, at which she'd eaten with her parents, was gone. The chairs were, too.

"Mom? Dad?"

No one answered. Her voice echoed through the house in a way that disturbed her. She walked from the kitchen to the living room, which was equally unfurnished and grimy. The windows were naked, with no curtains, and one pane was cracked down the middle; a triangular shard of glass was missing. She looked down and saw it on the floor beside the small rock that had probably knocked it loose.

Mary sat down at the foot of the stairs. For a brief moment, she wondered how long she'd been up there, how long she'd been writing. When was the last time she'd thought about anything but her stories? She knew there was a whole world outside, and some part of her thought she should go outside and see it. But then the phrase—those seven words—came back to mind, like a body bobbing up to the surface of a lake. She could feel it twitching, swelling like a blister about to burst. The story was almost ready to be told. And she knew that, as long as there was one more story to write, she would do it—no matter how much it hurt. She climbed the stairs, a smile on her face.

Opening her eyes and pushing the quilt off herself, the dream wafted away like steam from a shower. She was too tired to keep sleeping. Mary sat up and dropped her feet to the bedroom floor gently, carefully, sweeping them back and forth in case there were turtles there. There weren't. She looked at her desk in the dark room. A little bit of sunlight was coming through the window. Her notebook and her pen waited for her, and she...and she...

Was this how it ended? After she'd turned all the dreams into—what? What did she turn dreams into? Entertainment for the public? Did she *care* about the public? But if she didn't, what did she care about?

A small voice, so quiet she had to strain her ears to hear it, said, "Us. You care about us."

And through the wall began a procession of people she recognized, going back in time all the way to...

When had this started? When she stood on stage at the age of ten to read a story she wrote to all the students in her school? Or even further back, when she was four and the faces began to appear and to talk to her, when she had discovered that she preferred being with them to playing with the sorts of kids her parents thought she should play with?

Had it all been worth it? Would this experience set her up for a different, more satisfying life? A life with a loving partner, a job that people respected, perhaps children and a dog because she knew she wasn't a cat person, and a picket fence somewhere in the country with a rocking chair on the porch?

When she put it like that, the answer was obvious. No. It had not been worth it. She had given up too much, and gotten too little in return.

She remembered overhearing the first editor she ever encountered. He'd been talking to a colleague and had said, "The inside of Mary's mind must be a very strange place to inhabit." And he and the colleague had laughed.

Well, enough was enough. She didn't need to put up with any more of this. She picked up her latest notebook and threw it in one direction, and the pen in another. There was a whole world out there, and she was going to see what it had to offer.

But when she reached the door, it was blocked. She'd created so many characters in her time that it shouldn't have been possible for every single one of them to stand in front of the door at the same time. And yet, that was what was happening. They muttered to each other, then pushed one of their number forward. A spokesperson. This spokesperson took Mary by the arm and led her—gently, but firmly in a way that suggested refusal wouldn't be tolerated—back to her desk.

The spokesperson smiled at Mary, a gentle and understanding smile. "I have an idea. Let me tell you about it."

ABOUT THE AUTHOR

Kelly Ennis has had a lifelong burning desire to write a novel. At twenty years old, Kelly has suffered from severe anxiety and learned to manage it with a number of tools and outlets. Writing has been an oasis that provides her with the ability to express her feelings and fears in various genres.

Welcome to Brookville is the first installment of a planned series that will extend some of the themes readers will explore in this book.

Kelly lives on Long Island, New York, and is also working toward becoming a yoga teacher. She is an active volunteer, supporting animals and children as they work through their own difficult times.

What does an author stand to gain by asking for reader feedback? A lot. In fact, what we can gain is so important in the publishing world, that they've coined a catchy name for it.

It's called "social proof." And in this age of social media sharing, without social proof, an author may as well be invisible.

So if you've enjoyed *Welcome to Brookville*, please consider giving it some visibility by reviewing it on Amazon or Goodreads. A review doesn't have to be a long critical essay. Just a few words expressing your thoughts, which could help potential readers decide whether they would enjoy it, too.

CPSIA information can be obtained
at www.ICGtesting.com
Printed in the USA
BVHW070330280121
598938BV00001B/43